PRELUDE TO YESTERDAY

PRELUDE TO YESTERDAY

Ursula Bloom

CHIVERS LARGE PRINT
BATH

British Library Cataloguing in Publication Data available

This Large Print edition published by Chivers Press, Bath, 1998

Published by arrangement with the author's estate

U.K. Hardcover ISBN 0 7540 3407 0
U.K. Softcover   ISBN 0 7540 3408 9

E 2

PART ONE

CHAPTER ONE

WHEN Julia came to think more about it she realized that the message had truth in it. She *did* know very little of the man she would marry tomorrow. She had been too much in love to ask questions, and within her there had been the full and abiding trust which sought few answers. Or was it the age difference that had held her back? (Daniel was thirty-seven to her twenty-one.) She had been sublimely happy in accepting his love, she had complete faith in him even if they had only met a few weeks back, and now, having read the letter which she had picked up from the mat, she knew it was true. Daniel *was* a stranger.

She replaced the paper in the cheap light brown envelope, studying the writing carefully, it was unfamiliar, then she thrust it into her handbag. Anonymous letters were vile, so Charles had always said (Charles was her father), one should never give them a second thought, but one *did* give them a second thought of course; that was the trouble! Julia was trembling now. The barb had pierced more deeply than she had realized at first.

The cottage was still with midnight. It stood

in the Weald of Kent near River Hill, with Sevenoaks over the crest of that hill, and ahead the blurred tangle of the Hildenborough lights. Charles had bought the cottage at the time when Julia's mother had died and the child was but ten years old; he had chosen it because he thought the thatched barn across the back courtyard would make an excellent studio for him. He was in love with the red-tiled façade of the Kentish houses, Julia also.

Her first remark had been, 'How glad I am we came here. I love it,' and she had never changed from that first ecstasy.

Charles and Julia (they had always addressed each other that way) were deeply devoted. If Charles was almost a great artist who had never quite reached the top line, half of the trouble was an ebullient impatient nature, something that Julia had not inherited, but a trait that made him so attractive. He was a big clumsy man with a bulky body, thick red hair and a florid face, quite different from the girl. One would hardly have thought they were related. He had never cared what he looked like, laughed about his clumsiness and wore peculiar clothes in an unusual way.

'Charles, you ARE awful!' Julia would say.

'And you, my sweet, are quite lovely.'

She was, of course. The curious thing was that she was exactly like her mother who had been a plain woman, but the replica in her

2

daughter was surprisingly beautiful. Pale and svelte, she had that light brown hair which for ever attracts the sunshine. Her skin was porcelain and very pale, but her eyes were clearly beautiful with the translucence of water, its clarity and a light grey-blue. Charles had always said that Julia was just like spring-time flowers. He said also that she was in many ways a child, for she had never grown up. She denied it hotly. One does at her age. But deep down in her heart she had the gauche feeling of incompleteness. Of youthful helplessness, too.

Just now Charles was abroad.

He had had a difficult commitment when he had undertaken to paint a Mrs. Tanner, who was a rich man's wife in Sevenoaks. 'I should never have taken it on, Julia; it was the money which tempted me (quite the basest reason, of course), but whilst we eat it is important.' He had wrestled all the winter with the portrait and he was one of those men who could never face up to a situation which had gone wrong for him. He rebelled against mistakes. 'She has a face like a tired pork pie; she's all bust and bottom, and that's no help either,' he had said with gloom, knowing full well that much of the fault lay in himself. Julia had tried to encourage him and vowed that it would be all right in the end. He so seldom failed. She remembered suddenly how he had thrown her a kiss. 'I love you when you encourage me, Julia. Flatter me and I purr.

Who'd want lands and proud dwellings like the Victorian song when he had a daughter like you!'

When Mrs. Tanner's portrait was wearing Charles to a frazzle there had come the opportunity to paint an eccentric Baroness in Innsbrück. She offered him a four-figure fee. Not only did he see money in it but the chance to escape wrestling with the present portrait, and if Mrs. Tanner was peevish that it was unfinished, that was just too bad. Off he went. He had sent two over-coloured postcards back and some white felt imitation edelweiss. No more.

The tension in the cottage during the trouble over this portrait had been worrying, and in one way Julia had been glad to find it suddenly free from the strain. Now there would be a chance to get on with the spring cleaning. A chance to read some of the books she wanted, to make herself a couple of cotton dresses for the summer on a well-worn sewing machine which had hiccoughs if it went over more than three pieces of material at once. She was not lonely, for she had Mrs. Hogg. Hoggie was a pet, perhaps the world's most inefficient daily woman, married to an ex-hedger-and-ditcher (always known as 'Him') and living in a shabby squat little plaster cottage just down the road. Hoggie was for ever on call. Julia did not mind sleeping alone in the cottage, she loved the

4

whisper of trees on windy nights, she enjoyed reading in bed comfortably without Charles coming in and insisting that she put out the light because she'd 'spoil her pretty eyes'. She was happy in the fulfilment of all manner of small domestic duties that had needed her attention, then quite suddenly spring came.

It was a superb Lady Day, bright with grape hyacinths and the thorn starry in the hedgerows, for the year was young and very forward. 'We'll get an early autumn, we will,' said Hoggie moodily.

'Never mind, we've got the spring now,' said Julia.

She stood at the window staring out on the beauty of the Weald, and realising that beauty can be far more cruel than ugliness, for where ugliness makes one angry, beauty makes one think. It awakens all manner of forgotten anguishes. She stood in the garden, wearing her old flannel trousers and the home-knitted too bulky jumper, and she stared out across Kent.

In her very early twenties Julia still retained the thin youthfulness of a girl just before maturity. Her breasts were scarcely formed, and she was almost hipless. Charles had once said she was made of lath and plaster like Hoggie's ramshackle little cottage. Maybe he had been right; it had made her laugh anyway. About her was that elfin suggestion of real loveliness which clings to childhood when womanhood has already come very close indeed. Perhaps her sweetest point was that she would never really grow up. Some people are born with an eternal girlishness. It had been the gift of the fairies at her own christening.

Today, with the new spring abundant about her, it seemed to be an eternity since Charles had gone away. Restlessness came to her. The desire to go away herself. It was a sort of craziness which is born of lengthening days, of first flowers and the warm scent of mother earth and budding wallflowers in the first hot sun.

I shall go to Stratford-on-Avon, she told herself.

Once on the proceeds of a very special portrait, she and Chales had gone there and she had adored it. She had a vivid picture of the spire of the Holy Trinity church rising out of a green mist of breaking willows, of a small town with crooked streets, and a wide but lazy river. She remembered the theatre and the beauty of the play; taking an old car and visiting little romantic villages left by the high tide of progress and untouched. She acted on the spur of the moment, something which perhaps she had inherited from her father, though until this occasion she had been unaware of it.

I'd love to go again, she thought.

Two days later she was there.

★   ★   ★

6

It could not have happened if Aunt Rosabel, not notably generous, had not suddenly sent her a birthday present of a comfortable cheque. Unused to money, it seemed wise to spend it, the girl thought, and on the strength of this she went to Warwickshire. The wind was painfully chilly when she got there even if the sun was bright. The first anxiety came when she found that the hotel where she and Charles had stayed before was full, for she had never entertained the idea that this could happen. A second one was depressing and had only a dingy bedroom which she did not like. The third was full again. Finally she got alarmed and took the one which a small guest house in an uninspired back street could offer her. She had stayed away from home so little that she was unaccustomed to the problems that a holiday could present. She had travelled here joyously, had driven from the station in an ancient taxi-cab, and had thought that it was all the spirit of splendid adventure. Now, as she unpacked, she became a little worried.

She had an acute longing for Hoggie's presence; her highly glazed round face with the smile, and the permanent aroma of kitchen soap and fusty bodice which lingered about her. She was not pretty. Charles had always said that on some Hawaiian beach where they liked them fat, maybe they would have found Hoggie desirable, but frankly he felt her female charms were nil, and could never imagine what 'Him' had seen in her.

Because Julia dared not contemplate spending the whole evening in the drab sitting-room with nothing to do, she walked out to get a ticket for the performance at the theatre. As she crossed the bridge with the wide Avon lying beneath her, all reeds and rushes, she saw innumerable swans in full sail on an April floodtide. Like lovely ghosts. The boats were bobbing against the landing stages making an exciting drumming sound, and they smelt acridly of new varnish, for this was the start to the season. It was a romantic river, and she went on and down Waterside perplexed to find blustering crowds here, a couple of charabancs and much that she had not remembered seeing in the little town before.

Memory, ever the convenient cheat, had forgotten all those cheap shops with their tawdry souvenirs. Then she remembered as they had travelled back, Charles mentioning that the place was just a patchwork quilt put together by a slatternly grandmother who had the additional disadvantage of being colour-blind. He had been so right.

She turned into the box-office and made her modest demand for a seat for tonight's performance. A slightly acid girl looked at her coldly, after the manner of a trained nurse surveying a dangerous lunatic. It was a withering glance. It had the power to cut right into Julia, herself not modern or sophisticated and easily crushed.

'We have no tickets,' said the girl coldly. 'There's never a seat left on the day itself'—and as though that settled the matter she went on attending to her manicure. It was a slack hour and she was fussy about her nails.

'But just something? Perhaps standing room? I—I just don't mind what it is.'

'Nothing is left,' said the girl enjoying being quelling.

Helplessness engulfed Julia. The thought of the guest house was upsetting, and if she did not get a seat she had nowhere else to go. 'I—I had hoped . . .'

The girl in the booking office attended earnestly to a difficult cuticle, and as Julia turned from her realizing the hopelessness of it, the man who had been waiting behind her, spoke. She had known he was there, of course, no more.

'I beg your pardon,' he said, 'but I heard what you said and I came here to return a ticket. The man who was coming to the show with me was recalled to London as his wife is ill. If it's any use to you, do please take it.'

Julia had turned round and faced him.

The man was dark, so sunburnt that she got the impression that he must have come home

9

from the tropics. He had shy eyes, a sensitive mouth, and was far better looking than anyone she had ever met before. She knew that instantly.

'You're very kind,' she stammered, and because she wanted the ticket so much, she opened her bag to find the money for it. He stopped her with a gesture. She had the quick premonition that he had noticed the shabbiness of the bag even though she had given it a most vigorous clean-up last night.

'I don't want money, please,' he told her. 'It's a pleasure to give it to someone who wants it so much. I heard what you said, you see,' and then, 'I'm afraid you'll have to put up with my occupying the next seat.'

She did not even think of that. 'But I must pay.'

'I couldn't take it. Don't make me hand it in—and to that girl, too!'—he made a little face—'Please accept it.'

She took it gauchely not knowing what else to do. It did not occur to her that it could have happened on purpose; she knew it was spontaneous, knew by his quiet manner, his shyness, and the gentle way in which he handed it to her.

'All right then. Thank you very much.'

'Good. Now let's go in together, shall we?'

As Julia saw the girl in the box-office staring at them a certain sense of triumph came to her

10

knowing that she was walking into the theatre with a man who she felt must be charming. The girl had seen his good looks, and had heard his quiet voice. Perhaps she also had noticed that he was gentle.

They went in and in a second were sitting talking together as if they had known each other all their lives. She told him that she had visited Stratford once before with her father who was now away in Innsbrück.

'Suddenly I got lonely in the cottage,' she confessed. 'I got a crazy desire to come here because it was such fun last time. But today the place is different. It seems changed with the cold wind and all those crowds.'

'The Cotswolds are chilly in spring, and the town does get packed but the theatre's always nice.'

'Yes, indeed.'

During the first interval they went out to have a smoke, and she stood by a great window which looked down on to the Avon, its loveliness shimmering in the moonlight. It was like some ethereal backcloth of drowned stars and rush-bound island, clasped by thickening willows.

She said, 'I wonder what sort of man Shakespeare was?'

'Very like everybody else, I expect.'

'Us?'

'Probably much like us,' and he laughed.

'*Like us*,' she thought, 'and this is a man

11

about whom I know nothing save that his name is Daniel Strong, and he appears to be rich and talks gaily of having travelled.' She knew that he was provocative because he was so different from the young men in the Kentish village. He was in another category, or was it that her feelings for him were in another category? She could talk freely about home and her life, telling him the idiotic simplicities of her own little world, and aware that he would understand and not laugh about them.

That night she could not sleep.

She had sat in the theatre side by side with a charming and sophisticated stranger of another world; he was a man considerably older than herself, but her devotion to her father had taught her to admire and understand older men. Tomorrow they had made arrangements to visit Mary Arden's cottage at Wilmcote. Tomorrow was another day.

She was stimulated by the stranger's poise and his grip on life. She liked his courtesy, and yet the stimulation left her with a sense of childish loneliness. As if she were almost more alone than she had been before.

I mustn't be silly, she thought.

*   *   *

Julia and Daniel visited Mary Arden's cottage standing back from the quiet road with fantail pigeons about it, and the air of '*I know a Bank*.' He drove her over in an expensive car, and she admired the clothes that he wore so well, the hacking coat, the dark red silk scarf about his throat which lent an added darkness to his hair. Today on the river she did not notice that he was reserved any more. He asked a lot about Charles and was amused at what she told him, for Charles was a very amusing man. He told Julia little about himself. His mother had died when his younger sister Clare was born, and recently at the death of his elder brother he had inherited Wetherley.

'Wetherley?' she asked.

He warmed then. Apparently Wetherley was the Queen Anne house which had been in his family's possession for many generations and was situated near Guildford. He spoke of it tenderly, almost as a man talks of the woman he loves. He admitted that as a young man he had not spent much of his time there. He had travelled. Madrid. Brittany. A *schloss* on the Rhine, white with wild cherry in springtime and dark with the *tannenbaum* later on. He warmed, then chilled again when Julia spurred on by her interest asked him eager questions. 'He is like a pimpernel,' she thought, 'shutting its petals before a storm.' There were a lot of what she and her father called 'pimpernel people' in this world, and she niched Daniel as being one of them.

13

Her small mouth puckered nervously when, realizing her thoughts, he reached out his hand and clasped her own as it lay on the red leather of the car seat.

'Forgive me, Julia. I must seem strange to you, but I don't shut up for fun. I'm older than you are. Perhaps you are spring and I am summer. It could be that way. When one is older one has more secrets to guard.'

'Have you secrets?' she asked curiously.

'Haven't we all?'

'I don't know. I haven't any, I don't think.'

'How lovely for you! How sweet!'

He told her about his experiences at Eton, Worcester and the Bar, though he had never practised. 'Perhaps I'm a rolling stone,' he said. 'A spoilt child, too much money.'

When he laughed his face changed, so that the infection of his spontaneous joy made her laugh with him. But she still knew little about him. Just Eton, Worcester and the Bar. Of his strong feelings for the house called Wetherley. She became piqued. 'Perhaps there is a girl ...' she thought.

That afternoon changed Julia, and she sent Charles an absurd picture postcard of the Grammar School, writing on it in another of those mad moments, *How did you feel when you fell in love?*

They dined together that night at the Red Horse Hotel, where Daniel was staying, and

14

after dinner walked back together to her guest house. The evening was warmer for the wind had dropped and when they came to the octagon-shaped tollhouse on the bridge there was the scent of brackish water, of sturdy marigolds and meadowland. Julia had the feeling that the beautiful anticipation of this moment had always been within her; she was approaching an hour that she had awaited all her life, though she had never experienced it until now.

Now of course she knew.

In the boathouse there was music, and the record was playing *Mignon*, it was an inquiry with all the gay buoyancy of springtime about it. Daniel stopped and they leant side by side on the iron parapet.

'How lovely you are, Julia!' he said. 'So little and so young. I envy your simplicity of outlook, because it is something that I have never had. I would not have believed that anyone could grow up and still stay almost a child.' He paused. She felt the pause to be embarrassing, and did not know what to do or say. 'You know how I am feeling?' he continued.

She couldn't lie about it.

'Yes,' she said, 'I know.'

'It is the most wonderful thing that has ever happened to me, meeting you and knowing that I'll want you for ever. Being so sure, because I *am* sure, my darling. I suppose I'm rushing my

15

fences, I don't know. It all sounds so mad, but you're so different from the other girls.' He paused again. 'I had a love affair before. I thought that was going to be so wonderful and it was perhaps the most cruel disappointment of my whole life. It changed me. You could change me back, Julia, you—you could make everything so different.'

She didn't know what to say.

'I'm difficult, I have shocking moods, they run in our family for one thing, and for another life has encouraged it. When I'm angry I go quiet. Let's admit it, the candid would call it sulking.'

A tic throbbed in Julia's throat, she took a firmer hold of the iron railing. 'I love you,' she said, 'It's no good pretending. I don't believe in people who pretend. I—I just love you.'

He lifted one of her hands and kissed it graciously, so different from Charles, who was boisterous in his kisses. She found the elegant gentleness of Daniel bewildering but fascinating.

'I love you too,' he said. 'We have only met for two days, but I promise you that I shall love you till I die. This is the sort of emotion that is not born of minutes but is timeless.'

She thought of the other girl who had disillusioned him. 'She disappointed you,' she reminded him.

For a second a look crossed his face, a pain, a

16

regret in one. 'I know. Don't let's mention it again, forget it. It is over now. Dead. I don't want to remember it,' and then, 'When can I marry you?'

She clung to the iron railing with the sound of the Avon lapping the stanchions of a bridge that was built in 1066; there was the smell of water and the sweetly persuasive music of *Mignon*.

'Don't say "this is so sudden",' Daniel urged her as he gave her hand a little shake.

She said nothing.

* * *

Julia telephoned Hoggie next day saying that she would not be returning until after the week-end and that she had met new friends. Hoggie had been turning out the sitting-room and was caught at a disadvantage.

'No boys?' she asked suspiciously. 'Some nice young lady to go walks with?'

'Quite,' agreed Julia, and rang off.

She was in that dizzy mood which could not answer the sort of questions Hoggie would ask.

They spent the week-end going places—Compton Wynyates, Kenilworth, and an expedition to Edge Hill. They made love. The emotion which had been almost a game on Monday suddenly had gone deep and possessed Julia. She was so deliriously happy that nothing else seemed to matter. He had bought her a little

17

ermine jacket to wear and the Cotswolds were
no longer chilly. On her hand was a sapphire
ring with shoulders of diamonds. They had
cabled the news to Charles, and he had cabled
back. He must be in funds, she thought.
*Good luck. Make the most of it. I'm having
fun too,*
was what he said.

*   *   *

On the actual eve of her wedding day, with
the anonymous letter in her hand, for the first
time Julia was brought up with a jerk. What it
said was true, she did know little of Daniel.
Once in their hurried and romantic engagement
he had said wistfully, 'There are things I ought
to tell you,' his sensitive mouth twitching, and
she had laid a finger on his lips.

'Please not, Daniel,' for she knew that he had
a memory which hurt him and she did not want
him to be hurt. 'All this is so beautiful that I
want it to go on for ever, and post mortems
could only spoil it.'

'It shall go on for ever. I give you my word on
that. No confessional. No revelations.' She
could sense his relief. 'I keep my secrets and you
keep yours, bless your heart.'

When she got home it had been difficult
telling Hoggie about it. Hoggie always
suspected men, particularly good-looking ones.

18

She said most of them were murderers. Funny things happened, didn't they? You had only to open a Sunday newspaper and then you knew. Yet in the end she accepted Daniel. If her dad approved, well there was no more to say was there, but she didn't see how he could know. She and 'Him' had been talking about it. 'Him' thought it was 'ever so fooney'.

Then Hoggie accepted it.

'Daniel, all this is so quick.'

'Why not when life is short? Spring is summer too soon, and the autumn is no good to any one of us. We can't afford to let the happy moments slip by—they never come back, do they?—and my marriage can't be soon enough for me. I thought of next Monday?'

She felt herself trembling. 'Next Monday?'

'In the local church at eight. Lunch at Wetherley and then on.'

'But Daniel, we hardly know each other, and I don't know your people, nor do you know mine.'

'That might be an advantage,' he said, his eyes twinkling.

'I have never seen Wetherley yet.'

'Wetherley is a wonderful place. I want it to be my wedding surprise for you. There's only my sister for you to see, and we don't get on well. Clare is a bit of cold fish I always feel.'

'What a horrid thing to say! Am I a bit of cold fish?'

'Of course not. It isn't horrid, because it is true. Clare IS a bit of cold fish.'

Julia loved him so much that she would have agreed to anything that he suggested. They would marry and fly out to the South of France. Perhaps after a while they would go on to Innsbrück and see Charles if she wished. She did wish.

They dined the night before the marriage in the hotel at the foot of Wrotham Hill, sole possessors of tomorrow's joyous secret which made it all the more enchanting. Julia would tell Hoggie just before she left for the church, and Hoggie would send a telegram to Aunt Rosabel and a cable out to Charles.

They dined by candlelight in a great mansion whose titled family had gone. They had been impoverished by the inroad of what is called progress, and all that remained to remind one of them was the crest carved over the ingle; it was a sad-eyed doe staring out with the threat of the forest behind her.

It was one of those unbelievable nights which had suddenly come into Julia's life, of stars and a young moon, of champagne and exotic food. Tomorrow they would belong to each other for ever.

When they left the hotel and came out to the waiting car it was already late, and they dared not delay on the drive back lest they broke the age-old superstition which insists that no bride

20

meets her groom on her wedding day itself until she gets to the church.

'It's late; almost tomorrow already,' she said in a startled voice, and in the valley she could hear the nightingale singing.

'Prelude to yesterday and to tomorrow,' he told her. 'From now on we spend all our lives together.' She clung to him, for now he seemed to be infinitely tender, and infinitely close to her. 'You must forgive my moods,' he whispered. 'They come, but they go. Never let the fact that once I suffered deeply (and for that suffering pay in those moods) upset our happiness or hurt you. If a strange me seems unapproachable, the real me will always love you.'

'It is just the shadow of yesterday?'

'That's it, my darling, and in it may lie something of the prelude to tomorrow.' His mouth quivered for a moment and the very dark eyes smiled. 'Memories linger, they die hard.'

They raced home and she left him almost abruptly to be within the scheduled time. She walked up the crazy path and as she did so heard the church clock giving the warning for midnight. She had achieved it just in time. She put the key into the lock and opening the door stepped inside just as Daniel drove off and up the lane.

The letter was there on the mat.

CHAPTER TWO

Julia knew instinctively that the letter boded ill. She had a strange kind of intuition about it as she stooped and picked it up. Her first thought was that it was one of those ill-written notes that Hoggie sometimes left saying that 'Him' was ill and she would be late in the morning. Yet when she looked at the cheap envelope, Julia realized that it was addressed in a writing that was entirely strange to her. She tore it open, her apprehension increasing as she read it.

Don't marry him. You know nothing about him, and you'll live to regret it.

The note was unsigned. It gave no indication as to whence it came, only the message that it carried. It must have been sent by someone close enough to herself and Daniel to understand how little they had met, and well aware of the plans for the morrow.

Julia did not know more than that he was a rich man's son, that he had been to Eton, to Worcester, and had also been called to the Bar. That he lived in a home which he adored and which as yet she had not seen, nor had she asked to see it. It could well be that the suddenness and the intensity of falling in love had

22

transformed her, and she was in the mood that would accept anything save suspicion of the belovéd. *You know nothing about him.* How shatteringly true that was!

She hesitated a moment, then folded the letter carefully and put it into her handbag, but a second later changed her mind, and she took it out again, tearing it into small pieces like confetti, and letting the bits drop into the waste-paper basket. Irresolutely. In bewilderment. Very much afraid. As she did so the clock in the village struck twelve.

She was asking herself who could have sent that letter. Not Hoggie, for she had never written so well; besides, as yet she knew nothing about tomorrow's wedding. Not Aunt Rosabel, who so seldom met her relations, having a 'thing' about them, and anyway would have thought anonymous letters quite shocking. The vicar, Mr. Lucas, who of course knew of the wedding though he was sworn to secrecy, would never have done such a thing. He was an inoffensive man, pale as a stained-glass angel (once Charles had said, 'Put a lily in his hand he could sit for Gabriel!'). No, most certainly it could not have been Mr. Lucas.

Anyway, when she thought more of it—and she kept on thinking about it—Julia came to the decision that the writing was a woman's, and was sure that it came from one of her own sex. Men seldom stoop to anonymity.

The contents proved to be far more worrying than she had originally felt. It would all have been so much easier if Charles had been at home, but she felt bereft. Dismally alone. She did not know what to do and had no one to consult about it.

Tonight Daniel had promised her that after a week or so in the south of France they would fly to see Charles in Innsbrück and visit the *Schloss* of the eccentric Baroness, which in itself would be something of a thrill.

Curiously enough Charles had not written much about the engagement, which was rather disappointing; he had accepted it with an expensive cable, followed by one very brief letter giving his permission and sending his love. Julia gathered that the Baroness and her portrait were being singularly troublesome. He said that she was as mad as a March hare. He could not come home for the wedding; anyway, he didn't suppose that they would want him that much, but for the moment there was too much at stake. Charles's financial arrangements were always airy-fairy, and the four-figure cheque was keeping him at the *Schloss*.

'If Mahomet won't go to the mountain, then the mountain must go to Mahomet,' Daniel had said only tonight.

Julia slept little and rose early to find that Hoggie had already arrived, and the breakfast was ready—coffee and toast, scrambled egg, the

24

real kind, not duck, to which Julia and Charles had to resort when they were really hard-up.

'It's a lovely day, Miss Julie; chilly, you know, but nice. Dangerous weather "Him" says; gives people the pewmonia.'

Julia drank the coffee, but the scrambled egg seemed too much for her, and when Hoggie was in the kitchen she tipped it out of the window and prayed that the wallflowers would not give her away. Maybe the tits would oblige; they sneaked most things.

She was upstairs again and drew on the pale-blue coat that Charles had sent her as a gift for today. She fitted the little flower cap of soft white flowers over her hair, and picked up her gloves. Almost nervously she looked at the familiar bedroom in which so many hours of her life had been spent, then came down again. At the foot of the stairs she called to Hoggie. The old woman came out of the kitchen, staring a little bemused from behind the gold-rimmed glasses.

'You're all dressed up,' she said.

'Hoggie, I've got to tell you. I'm going to get married this morning.'

'Get married? Whatever for? And with your dad away from home. Whatever will he say when he gets back?'

'He knows it's today, Hoggie.'

'And I shan't see you get married?' Her little old face puckered.

'Hoggie, it's all right. There'll only be four of us; you have to have two witnesses, you see. Don't worry.'

But she was worrying. 'I was crocheting you a cushion cover,' she said, 'in yellow and green; ever so nice. It won't be ready in time. What'll I do?'

'You'll go on with it, and when it is ready bring it over to me. I shan't be that much far away.'

She heard the sound of the car coming up the lane, and as she listened she knew that she and Daniel would meet before they did at church. Did the old rules really matter? she wondered as she turned to the door.

'For the moment, good-bye, Hoggie dear. Look after everything for me.'

'It don't seem right,' was all Hoggie could say.

She ran out to the car and leapt into it, for she had the idea that Hoggie might follow her and she wanted to avoid that. Neither of them said a word as the car moved along the April-wet lane, turned to the right where it grew weedier, with the untidy verges and the thorn starry and white.

'All right, darling?' he asked.

'Quite all right, but a bit scared.'

'It won't take many minutes, and anyway I'm there, so don't worry too much.'

One thing was certain. She must never tell

26

him of that beastly letter.

They got out of the car and together walked up the path lined by damp yew trees to the door itself, where Mr. Lucas was waiting for them. ('Put a lily in his hand and he could sit for Gabriel,' was what she remembered.) Beyond him she caught a glimpse of the dark-red vestry curtains and the black fleur-de-lis stamped on them. Then she saw that someone had decorated the whole church. It was arranged as though for some fashionable marriage ceremony, radiating the glory of Easter lilies and white forced lilac in thick tassels of blossom. It is Daniel, she thought; he thinks of everything.

She was now too dazed to be aware of very much more until she came into the vestry with the ceremony over, holding his hand. The vestry was small and intimate; it smelt of rancid candle-grease, of fused matches and sacramental wine all in one. It was the little church that she knew so well, but the vestry was a strange place to her, and because of that she found it confusing. The excitement and the fear of the moment—for she was afraid—made her sensitive to atmosphere, and she disliked the smell of this place. She saw the register laid open on a small table, and she signed the place that Mr. Lucas indicated to her, her eyes blurred with tears which she believed to be happy ones, almost as if she was unaware of the significance of this particular signature.

27

Mr. Lucas gave her her copy of the marriage lines in the accepted manner.

'I do so hope you will be happy, Julia,' he said shyly, for he always found it particularly difficult to say the right thing when he knew the bride so well.

'I'm sure I shall be, thank you.'

'I hope so.'

He stood there smiling a little whimsically, a man in the forties, amiably friendly, but with his face showing signs of a life of singular hardship, for poverty had made times difficult and he always found it trying making ends meet.

The couple walked out of the familiar church with the *Agnus Dei* carved over the little porch, and looking up at it, Julia remembered Charles's cousin who, when she was shown it, had said, 'Oh yes, did she live here?' It was absurd that such trivialities should strike her at this particular moment of her life. Somehow she had thought that when she came out of the church the whole world would be changed, yet it was exactly the same as it had been an hour ago. Bird-song in the lime trees, the sun rising with a pleasant warmth, and may trees thickening.

She clutched the marriage lines and sat down in the car by Daniel's side. He drove away quite sharply, out of sight of the church, for instinctively he knew that was what she wanted; then he slowed down, still in the weedy, untidy lane.

'I love you, darling. I'll do everything in the world to make you happy. Do always remember that.' He seemed to be warmer to her than he had been before; there were no barriers, nothing between them, and she knew that she could open her heart to him.

'Daniel, I'm so scared.'

'Of course you are. I imagine that all brides are scared; they call it bridal jitters, didn't you know?' and he smiled. 'Don't let it disturb you. If we have got one another then all is well.'

The way he said it gave her the happy feeling that already they belonged. 'How sweet you are!' she whispered.

'We'll be at Wetherley in time for lunch, and I know you are going to love the place. But Wetherley will have to be my second love now that I've got you.'

'I shall never eat a thing at this lunch, because everything will be so strange. Even the house. I shall not realize that it is really and truly my home. Then there is your sister Clare! Is she alarming? The very thought of her makes me shiver.'

'Wetherley itself is sheer heaven; nothing to be afraid of but rather like meeting some gracious lady out of the past. Clare can be remote, I grant you; that trouble runs in my family, I suppose. We're all offhand at times, but she will have the good manners to make it easy for you.'

It seemed that Julia had already crossed the first threshold, but before her lay another one, and she recognized it. The complete depth of her joy in Daniel made her content, and he held her hand as the car went quietly along. She could forget the letter of last night. That was yesterday and this was today. Today was the only thing that mattered.

As they gained speed she opened the registration form which had lain so carelessly in her lap; she did it if only for the delight of seeing both their names linked in the most intimate association of all. 'Julia Trent, spinster'—somehow she had never thought of herself as being that. 'Daniel Mark Strong, widower.'

Widower!

She could not believe the word that she saw written there. Some mistake must have been made, and it wasn't true. She came out of the sense of bewilderment into the startling clarity of brilliant day, and she heard herself gasp.

'Daniel!'

'Now what is it, my sweet?'

'You never told me that you had been married before? You never said a thing about it.'

He slowed down and she could see his hands clenching the steering-wheel so that the knuckles turned almost white. 'But of course you knew, Julia. It's no secret. I was married when I was twenty-five.'

'But I didn't know. I had no idea at all. How could I have had?' Then, a little ashamed of her own distress, 'She—she died?'

'Yes,' he said. No more. The way that he said it gave her the impression that her loss had hurt him badly, and perhaps that was why he had never mentioned her to Julia. She was ashamed that she had been so surprised. She wanted to help him, to make it easier, and very gently she spoke again.

'Wouldn't you like to tell me something about her? It—it came as rather a surprise, you see.'

He made no attempt to help her. He said nothing, and this reluctance dismayed her. She was aware of a pulse beating in her throat, and when he stayed silent the throbbing increased quite unpleasantly; after a second she went on again almost desperately.

'Daniel, what do we do about this?'

It was shocking that until this moment they had been so happy, so sure of each other, so secure. Now it was like a fog descending on a November street in London, a thick wall of it seemed to have come between them.

'I'm sure I did tell you, Julia.' He said it almost coldly, his casualness overdone, so that it frightened her. 'It all seems to be so long ago. Anyway the marriage did not work out. It was very unhappy, nobody's fault, but just that— very unhappy. She had left me before she died.'

'Oh, Daniel, I wish it had never happened.'

31

Still he was silent.

Julia got the impression this was all he would tell her, at least for the present, and she did not press the point for she felt too hurt and too shy. His manner indicated that if she asked she would only be hammering on a barrier which would remain for ever between them. A previous wife! She had never thought of that. Why was it he had not mentioned a first wife to her, for she was certain in her own mind that he had not. She would never have forgotten such a fact. Now, whilst she searched for words into which she could put the question she wanted to ask, the opportunity passed, possibly for ever.

She forced herself to believe that he was excusing himself by pretending to have told her, and decided that she must be patient, though the shock of it all had left her utterly frustrated. She was exhausted by her own emotions.

The Weald of Kent lay before them, for they had travelled fast. The April morning broke with the full beauty of pale springtime, the shimmer of sunlight on apple blossom in small gardens, and on borders where those stocky little first flowers were colourful. Seeing them Julia spoke impulsively.

'It was nice of you arranging to have those lovely flowers in the church.'

'I thought maybe you'd like them. They made it rather special.'

'I adored them.'

32

'I felt white lilac was the thing.'

'It was beautiful, Daniel, quite beautiful.'

The other woman, that unknown first wife, had receded a little from the picture by the time they came to the sandier soil beyond Guildford, the city on their left, and on the right a patch of gorse already ablaze and open where later in the year the heather would streak purple.

'It's beautiful country,' she said.

'I love it. We shall get to Wetherley early, with time to see the garden. I've got plans for making a new rock garden there. You'll like the horses. Clare loves animals and will want to show them to you.'

Julia said 'Yes' uneasily. Had she rushed things? Too much in love perhaps? She felt uneasy, even deeply troubled at moments, and so helpless with it as they travelled on through country overrun with dense rhododendrons, the pine trees beyond, and the broom bushes rising. He should have told her! Of course he should have told her!

'We're almost there, Julie. It's your home, ours together, and I do want you to love it as I do.'

'I'll love it.' She resisted the absurd idea of asking, *Did she live here with you? Did she love it, too?*

They turned in at the gate and began to travel up the long drive that led to the house itself. Rooks cawed in the trees. The park lay to the left smoothly green with the newness of the season, and soon she saw the great calm pool which Daniel had spoken of and which lay before the façade of the house, in June spattered with white lilies, in autumn sprayed with a fine grey lace of mistiness. Then in another moment she saw the house itself, a mature line in warm red brick with the tall Queen Anne windows, and over the main door a fantastically lovely fanlight pursuing its own extravagant pattern.

'Daniel, how beautiful it is! How really lovely!'

'It's pretty good.' He was enthusiastic now, like a schoolboy, and not older than she herself was; he laughed, his nose crinkling with it, and the sound was carefree and infectious. She felt that they had rounded the first corner and the previous wife was forgotten in the admiration for the house. 'Yes, I AM happy,' Julia told herself.

The car stopped and Daniel sprang out, impulsively eager to show her everything, and the vivid contradiction to the reserve that he had shown such a short time ago.

'We're home at last, Julie darling, and bless you.'

She was slower in getting out of the car, for her hair blew across her face like a veil as she took off the little flower hat. They stood hand in hand for a moment admiring the pool, with irises springing up at the sides, soon to be flaunting yellow or pale amethyst, and the faint red shimmer of carp just below the surface.

'How beautiful it all is,' she said.

Wetherley gave her the feeling of complete peace, of something that she had not expected to find here, especially today, her wedding day, when she felt so strange, so shy, and somehow so vague about life in general. As Daniel had said, the place was gracious. It had atmosphere and was itself an elegant hostess waiting to welcome them.

She turned back from the pool and saw that the hall door was opening. A woman stood framed in the lintel with the exquisite fanlight above her.

'It's Mrs. Marriner,' said Daniel. 'She keeps house, and has done so for some years. Mrs. Marriner, this is my wife.'

Julia ran up the flight of steps to her, holding out her hand. The woman must be quite old, she thought, at least forty-five, smally made, almost to thinness, with tense pale lips and searching eyes. Her hair had begun to grow sparse and was scraped back unbecomingly yet was immaculately tidy. She carried her hands clasped together on her stomach, and Julia could see that they were beautiful hands like white flowers. Yet the woman herself gave the impression of being a character from Dickens; almost as if she had stepped out of one of his books. The dress she wore was a period piece of black silk, which made no attempt to pursue any set fashion but which clung to her scant figure whilst a small white lace collar lay at the base of her throat. Perhaps it was the intense whiteness of that collar which gave her skin a jaundiced appearance, and emphasized a certain remoteness about her.

'Good morning madam'—she spoke almost tonelessly—'lunch is almost ready, and I have put the drinks in the library.'

'Come, Julie.' Daniel reached for her hand, and together they went inside like children. If she felt the chilly eyes of Mrs. Marriner upon her she hardly noticed it, for now she was enchanted by the sight of a minstrels' gallery round the wide hall. She got the impression of large ingles, one at either end of the hall itself, of rugs in mosaic patterns, red and rich, yellow, black and gold. Of Jacobean furniture and of beauty. No wonder Daniel loved this place, and how much Charles would enjoy it, too! He always adored old furniture which had a tale to tell, the glow of Sheffield plate, silver with the underlying warmth of copper.

'Oh, Daniel, it *is* all so lovely.'

'Come and see the library, for that's my favourite room. I don't use the big dining-room which Clare admires, but the library has always had great charm for me. I want you to feel the same way about it.'

'I'm sure I shall.'

36

Again he almost ran with her to the library, hand in hand. The moment that the door opened on it she knew that she did share his affection for it. Although the walls were lined with books, a style she had always disliked until now, these were in deep imperial colours, gaily patterned in gold, so that the room glowed with them. The carpet was dark blue and very thick, whilst the room opened on to a terrace where in summer she knew they would breakfast. They stared out across the valley on to the Hog's Back itself.

Daniel was triumphant.

'I knew you'd love it, darling. I just KNEW!' Eagerly he pointed out different pieces of furniture and the colourings that he most admired. 'Before you meet Clare you'd like a wash? I suppose she is in the drawing-room, being the grand lady, and determined to do the thing properly. Come upstairs and I'll show you the way.'

'Daniel, it's all so exciting!'

They went up a side staircase and on to the long corridor which ran the length of the first floor, again thickly carpeted so that there was no sound as they went. He opened the door of a far room.

'This is all yours, Julie, my darling,' he said, infinitely proud of it as she knew by his tone.

It was larger than any bedroom she had ever seen before, the ceiling delicately painted with almond blossom and the floor covered by a huge light carpet giving the impression of a mossy glade with little springtime flowers in it. She could see through an open doorway the matching bathroom beyond.

She went to it and washed her hands, grateful for the comfort of warm water and sweetly scented soap. This gracious house could give her the gratifying sense of leisure. It seemed that almost too much had happened today! The morning had been more crowded with events than any other, and she had become conscious of a sense of tiredness quietly creeping over her.

When she came back into the big bedroom it was to find she was alone, and going to the windows she looked out across the Surrey valley to the Hog's Back, a view to which she was going to become accustomed and always attracted.

Standing here she wished that she could bring herself to forget the letter of last night. It was not that she resented the previous marriage; it was that she could not understand why he had not mentioned it to her. The thought of a first wife had been totally unexpected and she trembled at the memory of her discovery. Yet the arrival at Wetherley had been comforting for the house inspired happiness, even though she had at first sight very much disliked Mrs. Marriner and the thought of lunch with a new sister-in-law was alarming. It was ridiculous to feel worried about a housekeeper who looked like a character from a Victorian novel, silly to dread meeting a sister-in-law who might turn out to be quite pleasant. She pushed back the brown-gold hair which had been cut in page-boy fashion and was uncurled. Once she had longed for thick curly hair; she had felt that the straight wispy hair was ugly though Charles had always told her that an artist loved it. It was entirely unsophisticated and she only hoped that Clare would not feel that lack of sophistication countrified and out of date. Now that she was married ought she to try to change her appearance? All her life she had worn loose slacks and jeans, or abbreviated skirts, jumpers she had knitted quite badly for herself, and she had not bothered too much. Her hair had been worn in a big tassel round her head, but of course she could have a perm. She could have constant 'sets', she could try to become sophisticated.

There was a gentle tap at the door.

'Come in,' Julia called automatically, and she saw Mrs. Marriner entering, those beautiful hands clasped together and poised as before on the high stomach.

'Is there anything you'll be wanting, madam? If there is, would you please ask me for it?'

'There's nothing thank you.' Then, with an effort, 'What a lovely house this is and how well you keep it.'

39

'Thank you, madam.'

'You have been here a long time?'

'Twelve years, madam.'

In a flash Julia knew that she must have been here with the first wife! Mrs. Marriner had served her, could tell stories of her and knew all about her. At this very moment she might be comparing the two wives, a horrifying thought. Modest, and without conceit, Julia felt that she could only come badly out of any such comparison.

'You must be very fond of Wetherley,' she said shyly, 'and of Mr. Strong, also.'

'Everyone likes Mr. Strong, madam, and Wetherley too.' All the time she seemed to be making the words quite meaningless, and perhaps her eyes were speaking the truth more than those anaemically pale lips. The eyes were harsh.

'It IS a beautiful house,' said Julia, again playing for time. The circumstances of the day suddenly seemed to become almost unbearable. They bore down on her and she was unable to throw them aside. Before she could stop herself she came to her point. 'You were here with the first Mrs. Strong?' and she tried to treat it casually, as though it meant nothing though perhaps it was the most vital question of her life.

Mrs. Marriner made no reply.

As far as she was concerned the question might not have been asked, and the silence was utterly horrifying. When Julia spoke again her own voice was unfamiliar to her because she was so scared.

'I must go and meet Mrs. Stephens,' she said. With no change of tone so that she remained utterly remote Mrs. Marriner said: 'Yes, madam. She is waiting in the drawing-room.'

Julia walked downstairs. Now she could not think why she had ever asked that question, save that on impulse it had sprung out and almost had asked itself. As she went she could feel Mrs. Marriner's eyes watching her go down the stairs. Homesickness possessed her. An innate fear and the sense of coming into contact with something that she herself was too young and too foolish to understand. She would have given almost anything to see Charles awaiting her in the hall; Charles, so big and bulky, with that grin of his and the confidence that his very presence could give her.

Daniel waited instead.

'Clare's in the drawing-room. We'd better get this over, so come along and see her.' He put out a hand, then suddenly aware of her pallor, the limpness that had come and the realization of tiredness, he said, 'Has something happened?'

This was the moment of opportunity, the time when she could ask for help, but she stayed silent because she could not find words. Suddenly he seemed much older than she was, and almost a stranger. 'Nothing,' she said.

'Nothing at all, Daniel.'

He accepted that, and they went to the drawing-room, which lay on the western side of the house. It was an L-shaped room, delicately papered in turquoise with soft amber satin curtains. On the walls there were portraits of his ancestors, the kind that Charles most disliked, for he called them 'the art-gallery types of puffed-up prigs', their gilt frames tarnishing, yet somehow this seemed to add to the loveliness of venerable age in this room.

Clare rose from a sofa to meet her. She might be only thirty-five but she looked considerably older than her brother and infinitely older than Julia, who was of another decade altogether. The shock of this confused the girl even more. Daniel had never seemed to be so much older, but Clare did. She was fair; the small thin face was lightly freckled, her eyes had flaxen lashes and she had colourless fair hair which gave no personality to her appearance. Her mouth was a little peevish, Julia thought, and she had the Roedean-Heathfield public-school manner.

'Dear Julia!' she said. 'Welcome to Wetherley,' but she did not kiss her. For a moment they just looked at each other, Julia aware of the age gap, her own childishness and her sense of fear.

'Wetherley's beautiful.'

'Daniel thinks it's heaven. How dreadful it would have been if you hadn't liked it,' and she giggled.

'But I do adore it.'

Julia glanced from brother to sister with the sense of being the odd man out. I must be very tired, or the strain has been too much, she thought, for this sense of limpness continued.

'I think lunch is ready, and if we have it early it gives you lots of time to get to the airport without rushing it,' Clare said. 'I thought we'd have it in the big dining-room. We want Julie to see the place at its best.'

For a moment Daniel flashed in a way that Julia had never seen him do before. 'The big dining-room?'

'Why not?'

'But you know how I dislike that room.'

Clare ignored his anger. 'It is the room for an occasion and after all your wedding-day *is* an occasion.'

She led the way with the manner of one who has won a battle. She was the polished product of this background, and Julia recognized that she had an assurance which she herself did not possess.

They crossed the hall again with the friendly minstrels' gallery and the gaily patterned rugs, and went to the far room, with Daniel coming behind them and scowling. Julia had seen his resentment, and knew that this was something that was outside a plan that he had made. Clare went on to the room and opened the door. It was

43

long and thin with a claret-coloured carpet, and pale curtains exactly matching the grey wall. It had great beauty. The refectory table was set for lunch as an old-time butler would have set it, with silver bowls of daffodils and fern, with grape hyacinths in the epergnes, more fern and the soft pink primulas that were forced in the greenhouses.

'What a wonderful room,' Julia said, even though she knew that Daniel detested it.

At the far end was a mantelpiece of pale pink marble beautifully carved and veined, like a human body, in a way that she had never seen before. Over it hung a lone picture. It was the portrait of a girl with red hair. She was standing there, wearing riding breeches and a hacking jacket, a black velvet cap in her hands. The exquisite head was flung back as she laughed and the tawny hair was loose. Her eyes were violets in a pale but glorious face, and she gave the impression that she laughed at some private joke of her own, something nobody else knew about, and never would.

Her beauty was commanding.

Julia knew that the picture must have been painted by a famous artist to give the inspiration of that lovely girl. There were autumnal leaves in the hedge behind her, and a chestnut tree with its huge crumpled yellowing fingers was thinnning. Nuts were bursting out of their spiked green covers; she could see them. Every

44

detail was magnificent, but most of all the girl with the inspiring beauty. It arrested one.

'How glorious that picture is,' Julia said, and she knew that it compelled her. 'She is utterly beautiful. Who is she?'

They had come to the table with the flowers in the silver epergnes, and the delicately patterned china. Clare spoke very quietly as she looked across at her brother. 'You told her?'

'Of course I told her.'

'I see.' Realizing that she had asked a question she should not have done, she glanced at Julia, then sat down in her place at table. Almost offhandedly she said, 'It's Theresa,' and offered Julia the toast. Quite deliberately.

Instantly Julia knew that the first wife had been Theresa.

'She's very beautiful,' she faltered, and it seemed that the violet eyes in the picture sought her out, searched her, and questioned her in some indescribable way. *Once I sat where you are sitting. Once I was his wife,* said the eyes. *I loved Wetherley, too.*

'She was the most beautiful girl I ever saw,' Daniel said in a sudden impulsive admittance, and she realized that his brow had gone moist. *He still loves her*, she thought, and was ashamed of herself for being jealous.

Yet not jealous.

'Yes, she is very, very lovely,' she agreed.

She tried to check the rising emotions within

45

herself, all part of the bridal jitters, she thought; part of everything that had preceded today, and had begun last night with that wretched letter. If the letter had never been, then she felt she would never have become so agitated. She wanted to forget it yet could not forget it; the memory stayed with her.

Perhaps every marriage was something of a shock; the shock of finding yourself bound to a man for ever. Would it have been wiser if she had known a little more about him? Once there had been Theresa here in this very house. Someone whom Mrs. Marriner and Clare both had known. She turned to the egg in aspic lying on the Wedgwood plate before her.

Last night there had been the letter.

Don't marry him. You know nothing about him and you'll only live to regret it.

The egg was not going down very well. She put the spoon by. After all, she found she did not want it.

CHAPTER THREE

JULIA and Daniel had to leave early if they were to catch the plane from the airport. Julia went back for her things in the beautiful bedroom which looked across to the Hog's Back. She lingered a moment. I'll love this place, she thought, for nobody could have felt anything else about the Queen Anne house, and the gentle atmosphere which was all part of it. I know I'll love it, just as Daniel said.

As she came out of the room into the corridor, she saw Mrs. Marriner waiting for her, almost like an illustration from *Jane Eyre*, in that fashionless dress with her hands clasped together.

'Is there anything more that I can do for you, madam?'

'Nothing more, thank you. We shall be home again quite soon.'

'Yes, madam.'

'Good-bye,' said Julia, much as a child says good-bye.

'Good-bye, madam.'

She came down the big staircase and saw Daniel and Clare standing at the bottom waiting for her; for some reason she got the impression that they had quarrelled. She hoped not. Not today anyway, for it was her wedding day. Maybe she was over-sensitive to atmosphere. Charles always said she was, and she wondered if they had been talking about her, about Theresa and that other marriage. Was it an omen that the name should be one that had always been her favourite?

Clare looked up. 'Ah, here she is,' she said. 'France will be so nice. It is just the right time of

47

year for the Côte d'Azur, and after that I understand you are going to Innsbrück to your father who is on visit there?'

'Yes, we are. It will be lovely, for I have so missed Charles.'

'He paints, doesn't he?'

'Portraits.' Julia was thinking of the picture of the girl which hung over the dining-room mantelpiece. 'You'll like him. You see, Charles is rather a wonderful person.'

'We'll be seeing him soon, Julie darling,' said Daniel, and he took her hand in his.

She loved the contact with his warmth, and hand in hand they went across the hall to the big door open before them. The sun fell through the fanlight, and Mrs. Marriner was waiting by the door in the shadows, and quite still. Clare's eyes followed them both as they went out to the car. There Julia turned back.'

'Good-bye for now,' she called, 'only for now,' and got into the Jaguar beside Daniel. He started the engine almost as though he knew how much she wanted to be away. He accelerated, and they went down the drive with Wetherley fast becoming a dim hazy shape on the horizon and the pool before it a mere smudge.

Then Daniel slowed down.

'I love you so much,' he said gently. 'So very, very much, my darling, and I know I'm difficult and today has been a worry, but don't fret about

48

anything for we've got each other.'

'I love you.'

Wetherley was no longer dominantly compelling; it had gone. Mrs. Marriner, silent, too quiet, too old-fashioned, and Clare, had faded from their lives. Even the thought of beautiful Theresa looking out of her picture at them was no longer important. Julia held Daniel's hand, and its glow seemed to thrill her. The car was turning now in the direction of London airport, and she knew that she had always dreaded the thought of flying, but suddenly and quite surely she realized that with Daniel it would be safe.

Almost as if he understood her feelings, he said, 'Forget today, all of that no longer counts because you and I are together for always, and now at last we can be alone.'

Of course she could trust him!

Whoever had written that absurd letter knew nothing about it; the fact that he or she had left it unsigned showed that he did not know. All the hard lines of today which at times had seemed to press right into her were now being smoothed out by his love and understanding; they had gone.

'I'm not going to be frightened, Daniel?'

'No, of course not.'

They drove into the great airport and it was like entering a new world. Charles had refused to fly out to Innsbrück as the Baroness had suggested, he had insisted that this was something he would never experience, and would rather burst than be sick into a paper bag. What an idea! Instead he had made his way down to Dover, crossing on one of the roughest days of the whole year, and not caring. One thing about the sea was that it offered every convenience for being sick into, he explained.

They left the car and went past a maze of stairs and dull rooms into a strangely impersonal one, Daniel still holding her hand. Here they awaited orders. The place was mechanical, the officials aloof, merely figures, not really people, and Julia thought with regret of the lame but friendly porter at the station at home. The station-master, too, whose great hobby was mending watches and sometimes he became so interested that he did not know if the up-train had come or gone or not. Anyway he didn't 'hold' with 'all them modern methods.'

At last they were called out, down the unending steps to the tarmac itself, and Julia saw the great plane ahead crouched like some fantastic grasshopper on the ground. They went up the gangway to the suavely smiling stewardess standing awaiting them, and checking their tickets with the notes she held in her hand.

Daniel pushed Julia into the window seat. 'It's all right, my sweet,' he said.

'I'm just a tiny bit scared.'

50

'You needn't be. The main curse with flying is that it is so appallingly dull.'

'It would be awful if I screamed.'

'People don't scream, and I don't suppose for a moment that you will break the record. It makes a most ghastly noise when they rev. up; don't let that alarm you for the actual flight is not like that. They have to test everything to the uttermost first and flying is very quiet in comparison.'

'How do you know?'

'I was a pilot.'

She turned to him almost sharply. 'How much more is there that I don't know about you, Daniel?'

'I'm not sure. I suppose most young men of my era did fly, and I liked the idea. I can assure you there is nothing to worry yourself about in this sort of aircraft.'

So he had recognized her doubts! The fact that he knew was comforting, but she was tired of secrets between them. Of making fresh discoveries about him, especially coming as they did after last night's letter.

The engine began to make a great noise, so much so that she could hardly hear herself speak. Then when she became more accustomed to it, or it grew quieter (she did not know which), she asked again:

'When do we start?'

'There are lots of things to do first,' and he

smiled. 'Have a barley sugar?'

The plane was taxi-ing down the runway with grey buildings, all equally dull, in the distance. Perhaps Julia was not really mechanically minded, and somehow the whole of the airport had appalled her by its coldness. It did not touch the heart like the friendly little station, the lame porter and the watch-minded station-master, who had once let a train crash through the level-crossing because he just hadn't bothered to open it!

'Oh Daniel, I'm just going to hate this,' she whimpered.

Soon now they would rise, and she was not sure that she could stand it. Then as she glanced at the airport beneath her she saw that a tree had become as grass beneath her foothold, a straggle of buildings had lost their walls and were only roofs.

'Daniel, what's happened?'

'It's as easy as that, my sweet. It doesn't mean a thing and all we have got to do is to wait till we get there.'

The plane swerved, one side almost poised on a wing; he saw her anxiety and instantly was comforting; she adored him. Already he knew her so well. She could not speak but held his hand, then in but a few minutes it seemed that they saw the first blue streak of the sea.

'We can't be so far already?'

'Flying is quick, Julie.'

52

'It—it's almost nice.'

'Of course it's nice. You'll love it when you are used to it. There is no need to be afraid.'

The stewardess brought them food. Russian tea, cream cakes of the kind she had never had at home, *foie gras* sandwiches. They were lost now in a cotton wool world of cloud and the sun coming through it gave it an enchanting silver iridescence. To Julia it seemed like a fairy-tale— one of the Cinderella stories of her childhood which had come true. Charles had always had a passion for fairy stories, he still believed there were fairies and scorned those who did not. 'Disbelievers are all lady mayoresses,' he had said once in a fit of spite, 'or women magistrates, which is much the same thing.'

It was evening when they came down into a world far warmer than it had been in England. A grey car awaited them, and Julia had to admit that this landing was pleasanter than getting down into some dirty old station; she did not feel in the least exhausted. Usually she tired easily for she had never been really strong, and any strain on her physique took it out of her more than most.

They drove along the Grande Corniche.

In that hour her life changed. She travelled under strange new trees, oleanders with their cream blossom, cypresses and eucalyptus. There was the scent of mimosa and orange blossom on the small orange trees, and the tangerines were fruiting. They dropped down into the town itself and the car turned into the exquisite grounds of the hotel. The Mediterranean came in under the windows, it was a blue sea spiked with dark *caps* and with no distance to it. The grounds were spacious, the beds full of flowers—cinerarias in their multicolours, clove carnations and riotous geraniums, whilst verbenas and heliotropes perfumed the air. Already the first roses were in bud.

Julia looked about her amazed, her hair clinging to her face and giving an elfin impression very truly that of a girl who had never grown up.

'I did not know there were such lovely places in the world, Daniel.'

'You'll love it.'

'I love it already.'

She changed into one of the trousseau gowns that he had sent her as a gift and they dined in a superb room looking out to the sea, with the sound of stringed music coming from the recess. Waiters admired her, for the French pay compliments with their eyes, they are enchanting. Daniel watched her opening up like a flower; changing against the sophisticated background of gardenias and champagne, of compliments and gay music.

'Sorry you married me?'

'Daniel, how could I be sorry? I never knew that the whole of my life could change so much.

I never knew that I myself could suddenly be so different. It's wonderful!'

'I knew this was the spot for you. Ahead of us lie weeks and months of happiness; years of it; we are the luckiest people in the whole world for life is ours, and love is ours, and everything lies before us. Did you know?'

She looked into those unbelievably dark eyes of his, at times curtains drawn on his innermost thoughts but now full of the depth of his emotion for her. She had been a little idiot to think for a moment that she did not know him. A little fool to become depressed by trivial passing moods, or by a stupid letter which no one had had the courage to sign. Even the thought of Theresa accusing her with those eyes of hers seemed to fade. Why worry about someone who had already gone for ever?

She said tenderly, 'Marrying you, Daniel, is the most wonderful experience of all.'

He leant across the table and taking her little hands in his kissed the finger tips with elegance. A passing waiter smiled; *'la grande passion'* he told himself and raised his eyebrows. It would be midnight before he could get out of this place to see Angèle, a *midinette*, a flirt, a naughty girl, but *charmante* for all that! He passed on to another table, mopping his hot face with the napkin, then replacing it about the dish.

'Thank God for you, my Julie,' Daniel was saying. 'I pray never to give you regrets. All I want is your happiness, and for ever . . . '

*　　*　　*

The Côte d'Azur gave Julia infinite joy.
Daniel became gaily amusing, as if he had not a
care in the world. He was so young with her, so
happy, and they lazed through life, learning
each about the other's personality, admiring,
and longing.

In Cannes he bought more clothes for her,
and if he was extravagant it gave him infinite
joy. He knew the shops well, exquisitely
arranged, small, perhaps with only one tiny
petit-point bag in the window laid on a velvet
cushion, or a single chemise delicately hem-
stitched.

They visited ancient *châteaux* in the
mountains, the *Salle Privée* in Monte Carlo, San
Remo with the dark red roses clambering
everywhere—never had Julia seen so many roses
all at once! They went to Grasse, where he
bought her perfumes at a quite horrifying price,
thousands and thousands of francs at a time, and
when she frowned he laughed at her.

'What is more you must use it all, Julie,
before we go home, otherwise the Customs will
be furious, and there really is no need to
economize,' he told her.

It was incredible.

Julia and Charles had lived on cheques when

56

they came and credit when they didn't. It had been life on a shoestring all the time. Charles had not worried too much because he was accustomed to it, but there had been moments when Julia had grown suspicious of strange men on the crazy path, with that look of stolid determination to get something at any cost, hanging about them.

In the first fortnight of marriage she had changed. A famous hairdresser cut her hair so that the tousled look left it and it became the *gamine* head of a child; a new make-up made her provocative. She had not bothered before—in the village nothing had mattered much—but the little more made the greatest change in her. She wore lovely clothes, and some of the apprehensions she had felt for tomorrow faded out in the completeness of today. She adored Daniel.

It would almost seem that they had left all fears behind them in England, and here were two people who had come to the south of France already very much in love, only to fall far more deeply so.

Only once did Daniel refer back to the life they had left in England. It had been very hot that day, and he lay reading a newspaper on one of the twin beds in their room. The orchid taffeta quilt was crumpled—he did not care—Cluny lace pillows were pushed casually aside. The room was painted in soft pink, and plaster cupids poised indolently over the doorway, whilst big french windows opened on to a garden rich with the scent of orange blossom. His shirt was open and his hand on Julia's as she squatted on the other bed to mend a petticoat strap.

'You knew so little about me, darling. How brave you were!'

'I knew enough to be sure that I loved you.'

'Marriage is for such a long time. You did recognize that?'

'I'm not afraid.' She flung down the mended petticoat and laid her face against his throat. 'I was only afraid for a moment when I got that letter.'

'What letter?'

'I—I suppose everybody gets one of them at some time or another; this happened to be my first one. It wasn't signed; it said that I knew nothing about you and must be careful.' As she said it she saw the sudden change in his eyes, a change instantly controlled, so that he became a sphinx. 'In spite of it I did marry you, Daniel.'

He got up from the bed, and going over to the window stood there looking out across the garden, with the orange and the lemon trees, the rippling colourful borders of cinerarias and the clove scent penetrating into the room. He took a cigarette out of his case rather slowly, lit it, and began to smoke it, and as she watched she saw that other man in him. It was the man she did not quite understand, the man who said nothing at all.

'There—there isn't something wrong?' she faltered uneasily.

He did not turn, but still stood looking out at the formal garden. Then after a moment he said, 'And after you got that letter, you found there were things you didn't know?'

She could not deny it; in her imagination the ghost of Theresa had come into this very room to point an accusing finger at them both.

'Yes,' she said.

'Probably you wonder how much more there is?' and his tone sounded bitter. She did not answer because she dared not, and at this moment she was hungry for the man she loved, the man who could lay his heart bare to her, not the one who was silent. After he had waited, he began again. 'I'm a queer sort of chap, Julia. I can't stand being asked questions, never could. It may seem hard but that is the way that I am made. I shrink into my shell, hide myself, cannot come out into the open and don't know why. One day maybe I'll conquer it. I don't know. But for the moment I love you and that is surely all that matters? Can't that be enough?'

'Yes, of course it's enough.'

'Then let's forget the rest.'

She wished he did not disappoint her, but he did. She and Charles had always led life without secrets. They turned back the pages together and never closed the book. This subject had cropped up at the end of the happiest fortnight of her life, the first precious two weeks of marriage. Maybe time would help, and he would come closer. He would understand. Soon she would be seeing Charles and he knew all the answers. 'He'll help me,' she told herself.

★   ★   ★

They flew next day to Austria.

This was the most exciting part of the honeymoon, the highlight, the time that mattered most. The flight was easy and quick, and the excitement within her stimulating. It was delightful to sit there with Daniel holding her hand, and as they flew she wondered if the wall between them had been just part of her imagination, something she had herself created, and matterless. After all, everyone got anonymous letters at some time or other, she had said to herself. Half the world married twice, and anyway Theresa was dead. The years had passed on, and Theresa was a ghost—no more—a phantom whom one dismissed at cockcrow.

Julia told herself that she must be the one to conquer her own apprehensions, and not let any of this hurt her deeply. That was what she had decided when they touched down in Austria. In the next few minutes there was the confusion connected with any landing, the Customs, the passing out to the waiting cars and then the drive through amazingly beautiful country and away. No wonder Charles had lost his heart to Austria!

'How wonderful it all is, Daniel!'

'The loveliest country in Europe.'

'Of course. I had no idea it was so perfect.'

Fir forests came close to the roadside, a shrine stood back, its canopy like that on an English lych gate, and the plaster Christ gleaming in the sun or glowing in the tree shadow. It might be only early May but here the flowers of summer were already blossoming; the large-eyed daisies, Canterbury bells in vigorous pinks and blues, chicory and gentians.

For the first time she saw the *Karwen del Grüppe* of silver-streaked hyacinth mountains with Innsbrück at their foot. The sun flashed on the snow, and before her lay the valley dotted with colourful houses, small but enchanting, their roofs held in place by pieces of rock set on them in an absurd fashion.

'You should have told me it was so lovely, Daniel.'

'I wanted you to discover it for yourself.'

'You knew I'd love it.'

'Yes, darling. I knew.'

Leaning towards him with the eager ebullience of the child who speaks before she thinks, Julia asked, 'Did you bring *her* here,

61

Daniel, and did she love it too?'

He looked at her with that sealed look of his. It made him inscrutable, and she knew that she should never have tried to break the silence. Instantly she was angry with herself for having tried to force his confidence, for having rushed out to meet him when as yet he was not ready to meet her. One day perhaps he would tell her all his secrets.

She sank back disappointed.

CHAPTER FOUR

CHARLES had gone to Austria delighted at the chance of earning a thousand pounds. His arrival at the *Schloss* had been disappointing. The Baroness's car had sped him there from Innsbrück, and it was considerably smaller than he had expected. Then before the door itself he caught his first sight of the Baroness. Oh, my God! thought Charles.

She wore a hacking jacket which had a resolute determination to rise at the back, a rough skirt and a Tyrolean hat. She carried a gun. As he descended from the car and bowed she approached and addressed him in guttural English.

'I have so much the delight,' she announced.

'I also, *gnädige Frau*,' said he, hoping this was

correct.

At this moment a flock of pigeons rose in a cloud from the courtyard behind them, and the Baroness seeing it, cocked her gun and let off a couple of barrels at them, then popped it under her arm again having hit nothing. Charles hated violent reports. He grabbed his suitcase as though it were a lifebuoy in some malignant sea and dashed into the *Schloss*. Oh hell, said he to himself.

It was a little later that he met Griselda.

No one had told him that the Baroness had married a handsome young rogue, who had given her a daughter and then had had the good sense to get himself shot in the war. The child of this flagrant marriage had great beauty, with a small pink face much like the July phloxes in a country garden. Charles, who had thought he was well past such foolishness, saw Griselda and fell in love. It was as simple as that. He had not believed that it could happen but it came on the moment and he succumbed to it.

If painting any desirable portrait of a woman so shocking-looking as the Baroness was impossible, he did not care. The fact that Griselda was almost Julia's age did not alarm him. She was just a sweet kid and he was young again in loving her. He might have thought that he had outstripped all the spontaneity of emotion; if he did he had been wrong, for now he found himself flooded by its fullness.

He told himself it would pass—it must do; when it didn't he was delighted, even though it might entail complications.

Perhaps he was fortunate, for he always boasted that fate was his friend and played into his hands, for Julia was having the same thing happening to her at Stratford-on-Avon. Once Charles had supposed he would be inordinately jealous when she married; now he saw it as the way out. She wanted to marry immediately; her letter was a schoolgirlish confession of a tide that she could not stem. No longer did the ghost of doubt pluck at his sleeve, the fear that questioned how on earth he would break the news of his own love story to the girl he adored.

The situation was solved for him.

They were married and happy; they were in the south of France and in bliss. They were flying to Innsbrück to see her father and the Baroness, and suddenly he knew that when they arrived he would HAVE to tell them, for the love affair was proceeding rapidly. Griselda would marry him, she said, but her fear was breaking the news to her mother. Her mother was a difficult woman; she flew into stormy passions (as though Charles did not know that one!). She was loud and vigorous and angry. Worse, as he was to discover, she had her own plans.

He found those at the very time that Daniel and Julia were preparing to fly farther to Innsbrück, it was one evening when Griselda had gone out to a ball, and he was left alone to play bezique with the Baroness.

She stopped playing. 'We 'ave the leetle talk, *ja*?' she asked, and about her there was the air of a lady approaching a crisis.

'Fine,' said Charles, who hated bezique.

'Life has the complex for me. I am the widow. *Ja*?'

'*Ja, ja,*' he agreed.

'I do not vish it so. I am the romantic. I prefer the lover.'

He looked at her; a vague distrust came into his eyes.

'When I do see the picture you make of me, I know,' she said with an appalling confidence.

'Do you indeed?' he asked, but he was not happy.

She tapped her robust bosom with a hand that was smothered in diamonds. 'I am free,' she said.

He looked at her. 'Fine,' he said airily, but he knew that his voice had gone slightly hoarse, for he was under a severe strain. What was she up to? The cheque she would be giving him was God's gift, the *Schloss* amiable, and Griselda a dream of joy, but what was actually happening now?

'I did say to myself no marriage never more,' she stated, then after a pause, 'but zat is not so. You are vonderful.'

Charles felt little hairs sticking up down his

65

spine and a spurt of eager perspiration to the brow. The truth dawned on him and the truth was utterly frightful. This woman saw in him a lover and he was already in love with her daughter and was waiting for a suitable moment to explain matters to her. This was not the moment. She smiled encouragement to him, and he had run out of words in which to state his case. At all costs he must not risk her going back on the cheque.

'Ven do ve tell the world?' she asked, and lifted her glass of port, her eyes smiling.

He began firmly. 'Baroness, I am a widower. I loved my wife and because of that would never think of taking another.' In the emergency he dared not admit that he was perhaps precipitating himself into an even worse crisis. Sufficient for that day was the evil thereof, and whatever happened he simply must get out of this. 'I shall never re-marry,' he said, and as something of a makeweight added another 'never'.

'I vill make you.'

'Don't you flatter yourself.'

Yet he knew that if she got down to it she probably would make it impossible for him to escape. He rose dizzily, and it was not only that rather bad port of hers.

'This has got to end, madam,' he said and blundered out of the room.

CHAPTER FIVE

Julia was in Innsbrück.

She and Daniel had dined together in the spacious dining-room of the hotel which looked across to the *Karwen del Grüppe*. It was lightly patterned in beech the colour of honey, and the carpets and curtains were of spring green.

'I suppose we couldn't drive over to the Baroness's *Schloss* and pay a surprise visit to Charles tonight?' she suggested.

'Why tonight, dearest, when I want you to myself? Tonight is ours surely? tomorrow is his day.'

'I was longing to see him.'

'You've got me,' Daniel told her and stood looking at her between tall candles in silver sconces with great bowls of blue gentians under them. 'You would not want to make me jealous before I ever meet your father?'

'How could you be? We have been brother and sister. He was always my big brother and such a darling.'

'I wonder if one can rush relationships that way? Now that you have a husband he will be just your father, I imagine.'

'I wonder. I can't imagine any other relationship. We have been so together.'

'Now you are mine.' He changed the subject

quickly. 'One day, darling, you are going to love me quite tremendously.'

'But I do love you, Daniel. I love you so very much now.'

He looked across the table at her and smiled fondly into her eyes. 'One day you will love as women love, for now you are a child. Did you know?'

'Charles once said I had the miracle quality of never growing up.'

'But you will grow up, one day. Then you'll be so happy. Then you'll be so wonderful my little one.'

They finished dinner and walked into the big reception-room beyond. At the far end a Viennese band was playing the alluring music of the Danube. They sat for a time on a great sofa with coffee, for the music was a tender accompaniment to the loveliness of this hour together. There seemed no barrier left, for she had surmounted it. Perhaps Daniel had been right and they had needed this moment with each other.

'All our lives lie before us, Julie.'

'I know.'

'Somehow I feel that this is a very special night before we go tomorrow to meet your father. I want him to see you happy. Maybe he will be changed.'

'Charles would never change.'

'Wouldn't he? One never knows. He sounds a

68

most attractive personality.'

Whimsically she said: 'Nobody could do anything but adore Charles. He isn't like anybody else in this world, and the queer thing is that it isn't awfully easy to describe him. He does the sort of things nobody else could do; he gets into jams and out of them again just as though they had never happened. He enjoys every moment of living. He is just Charles.'

'Not like I am?'

'No, Daniel, Charles isn't a bit like you, but perhaps the fact that you are such opposites is what makes me love each of you so much.'

'You're sweet,' he said.

'Daniel, you can trust me.'

'I know I can. Do you find me difficult at times?'

'Just a bit.'

'Poor pet! There've been things in my life, embarrassing moments I suppose you'd say. It's no good talking about them, for anyway they are all over now, but sometimes they make me want to sneak out of the world for a bit. One can't kill memories. I suppose that is why I stay behind a barrier.'

'Did you always?'

'Oh no.'

'It happened when—when the other happened,' and she thought he meant Theresa. It was all wrong that it should be so complicated talking about Theresa, a ghost whom she had never seen, yet a very real and formidable presence who seemed to stand between herself and Daniel. 'Yes, yes, it happened then.' For a moment it was almost as if he would tell her, then his tone changed. She saw his face change with it.

'Daniel, let me come behind that barrier with you. Darling, please don't shut me out.'

'Perhaps one day.'

'But why not now?'

'No, not now,' he said.

The orchestra was playing Strauss's *One night when we were young*, and as she listened she knew that she would always remember this provocative melody as being part of themselves. Like *Mignon* at Stratford-on-Avon, standing by the river on that very particular night when first they had been quite quite sure that they were in love. He read her thoughts.

'I love this music, too. We'll keep it and make it ours, shall we?'

'For always.'

'Yes, darling, for always,' he said, and held her hand fondling the fingers with his own. Very gently and with infinite love for her.

They sat on late and at the far end of the room other people were dancing, yet tonight Daniel and Julia did not dance, but were happy to sit with each other, talking in half whispers. She almost wished that the night would last for ever.

Much later they went to bed.

It was already the new morning, and the stars hung over the sprawling valley like a sequined canopy into which the sharp white points of the *Karwen del Grüppe* spiked gauntly. She stood at the window looking out at it, surprised by its stark beauty and amazed also at her own life, which had changed so completely; puzzled too at the mystery of something which lay behind Daniel, something which she could feel all the time yet never actually touch. It wasn't that she minded his having married before; she kept telling herself that this was not jealousy. Theresa had been so beautiful that any man would have wanted to marry her for her loveliness alone, and already she had gathered the impression that she had been a gay provocative person, someone who had great charm. What she felt about the present situation was not annoyance.

It was that she wanted to know more.

Daniel was holding something back from her, and going to infinite pains to conceal it completely. It was not the fact that he had been deeply in love with Theresa—there were moments when she almost doubted that he had been in love with her at all, most certainly during the last part of the marriage—it had been something during the last part of the marriage— it had been something quite different.

One day I shall know what it is, she thought, one day everything will be all right and, knowing, I shall understand. There was no need to be jealous of Theresa, and of that one point she was quite, quite sure. She went back into the room drawing the curtains across the view of the valley. She sat down at a highly modern dressing-table in honey-coloured wood with a huge mirror on it, and she started to brush her hair.

It is today. The day when I shall see Charles again, she told herself.

*   *   *

They drove over to the Baroness's *Schloss*.

The arrangement had been that they were to arrive in time for *Mittagessen*, and for that meal Julia prepared. Knowing how much Charles adored colour she had chosen her clothes for this occasion with deliberation. When she came to think about it he had never seen her before in what she would have called party wear. She had been the *gamine* creature of the cotton frock, the old slacks and the lumpy sweater that she had knitted for herself. If he admired pretty clothes on other people, certainly he had never associated them with her. But that had changed and for the first time he would see her in a quite different kind of dress.

She wore a cyclamen-pink suit and the deep coral earrings and bunchy necklace that Daniel had bought for her at a small antique shop in

72

Cannes. It had looked quite simple, almost inexpensive, yet she knew that it had been a shattering extravagance.

They got into the hired car and drove through the most exquisite countryside. All the time the mountains enclosed them, but far away, so that there was no feeling of claustrophobia. At one moment a lane was a drift of Canterbury bells in blue and pink, great fat spires of them, vigorous and sturdy in growth, and in yet another the great yellow-eyed daisies lay all about them, much like fallen stars. There were the clustering trees, in places woodland coming right down to the verge edge, and the resinous scent of cedar and of pine. There were the picturesque little shrines, with dying flowers grouped at the foot of some dying Christ, with a lych arch above them, and the deep violet shadow of the midday cast by it.

'This is our journey to adventure,' Daniel told her, laughing. 'You don't seem to realize that I am in the unhappy position of being the son-in-law approaching Papa for the survey. He may hate me.'

'Charles has never hated anybody in his life,' said Julia, though she recalled Mrs Tanner, who had been such a nuisance over her portrait. She had fostered the idea that Charles had only to say the word and the picture would be at Burlington House, to the envy of her friends. Charles would never have said any such word, and had he done it would have cut no ice.

'He may hate me. Men get awfully jealous of a son-in-law, and you two were awfully attached.'

'And now I'm married.'

Daniel laughed again. 'That is exactly the bit that he may detest. Stand by me, darling. It *could* be hard going.'

She said, with little idea of how near the truth she came: 'By now Charles will be submerged with the Baroness, her daughter Griselda, and the *Schloss*. He is able to plunge himself into a new atmosphere that way and surprise the world. Of course I'll stand by you, but I shouldn't worry.'

She held his hand as though she wanted only to help him. This was perhaps one of the great moments in her life, for the meeting of Charles and Daniel had got to be successful. They were the two people whom she loved most, and they must become friends. Daniel mustn't turn shy. He must not shelter behind one of his moods, and she told him so.

'Of course not. Anyway, I'm not that much afraid,' he said, when she mentioned it to him.

They were early.

It must have been that somebody's watch was wrong, and not for a moment would Julia have admitted that purposely she had done this solely with the idea of seeing Charles sooner. She was so excited at the thought. They saw the little *Schloss* coming into view. The Baroness was flying her personal standard from the main tower, an idea she had picked up on a visit to England, when she had been impressed by the flood-lit standard above Buckingham Palace.

'It's rather pretty,' said the girl, aware that at the thought of meeting her father again she was once more becoming *gamine*.

'Yes, but that flag. What does it mean? Who is this old Baroness anyway? They are ten a penny in this part of the world, I should have said, wouldn't you?'

'I just don't know.'

Charles had intended coming down the drive to meet their car and so avail himself of the privilege of having the first few minutes with them without an audience. With this purpose in view he had stepped out of the *Schloss* and had started across the lawn. Griselda joined him. It is true that he found this trying, for he was realizing more and more that he should have warned Julia that he was secretly engaged and not have left everything to the last minute. Although this was his usual form of retreat on the principle that 'it's bound to be all right, for God is pretty good to a chap like me!' he had been caught unawares. There was also the very ominous knowledge that the Baroness had set his cap at him.

He took Griselda's funny little hand into his own. It had never a pucker on it, not a wrinkle or an upstanding vein. Just one little adolescent wart which was sheer joy. What a darling she was!

'You are going to adore my Julie, for she is just your sort,' he said, bright with optimism, whilst deep down within him there were some alarming heart-prickings. For Julia married might be an entirely different story. She'll never change, he thought; yet she might, common sense reminded him.

'If she is like you, of course I shall love her. We shall be the greatest friends.'

He swung her off her feet into his big arms. She was as light as a child and he was strong with the emotion which the affair had reborn in him. He kissed her again and again, just as Julia's car turned up the drive and the two occupants sitting in it could not fail to see what was happening. Daniel's first glimpse of his new father-in-law was of a man in a crazy mood. Julia instantly recognized that Charles was enjoying himself—she had quite expected something like this—yet on second thoughts she fancied that she detected a new quality about him, something that she had never seen in him before.

She yelled to the driver of the car to stop, and before it was completely still had sprung out of it.

'Charles, Charles,' she called, and regardless of Griselda flung herself on him.

He wore strangely different clothes (he had

76

not been able to resist an impish impulse to go Tyrolean), but he looked splendid in them, she told herself, boyishly amusing.

'Julie, my own darling!' and because it had to be now when he felt brave because otherwise he would never be able to do it, 'I'm in love, too. Both of us got the same idea at the identical moment, and that's pretty wonderful, isn't it? Both of us are going to live happily ever after, for this is Griselda.'

His gaiety was a tonic. Yet he did not deceive his daughter entirely. She knew that he really had changed, or had she? One of them, most certainly. This was not the old familiar Charles, the prop behind her entire life. He was being rather foolish falling in love, yet he had a right to his own happiness. It was not her nature to be jealous, only a little regretful, and for this one moment it threatened to submerge her own longing for his happiness. Instantly she quenched it, for it was ridiculous.

'Hello, Griselda. Lovely to find it this way. And this is Daniel.'

'Hello,' said Charles, but awkwardly.

Here were four people all entirely different natures, who had taken each other by surprise in the drive of the *Schloss*, with the enormous mountains beyond them, and Innsbrück lying low in the valley beneath them. Julia swallowed anxiously.

'Hello,' said Daniel.

Griselda looked quite charming, but was very young, of course, and rather shy. She hung back a trifle as Julia tried to tell Charles all about the marriage. How benign Mr Lucas had been! How it would have amazed poor old Hoggie, who anyway thought all men were cads! Julia talked of the honeymoon, of the rare beauty of Wetherley and how much he would love it.

Even as she talked she felt a sort of faint despair that she could not get her father alone and to herself. He was the one man in whom she could confide her doubts about Theresa, dead and gone, and that wretched letter lying on the mat the very midnight of her marriage, and which was NOT dead and gone but which lived in her heart and would not let her be.

All along she had been telling herself that when they met she would be able to tell him everything, and he would help her. He was just the one person. Yet now she felt the ground gradually slipping away from under her feet, for he had changed. This was not the same Charles. Or she was not the same *gamine* daughter, and somehow she had never imagined that this could happen to them?

They were chattering when the Baroness came out of the *Schloss* to greet them. Although it was a very hot day she wore a thick tweed dress, with a surprising number of gold chains looped about her large bosom drawing attention to a portion of her anatomy which would have been better left alone.

'Vell,' she said, 'vell indeed! *Ja*! Ve all meet togezzer. It is the great delights.'

She was so beaming and so well pleased with herself and the world about her that Julia, only too anxious to be friendly, broke into ecstasies about the news. With childish excitement she said: 'Isn't it wonderful about Charles and Griselda? When is the wedding going to be?'

The Baroness was a remarkable woman.

She did not quiver. None would ever know that at this instant the dream of a personal romance dispersed into the thin air, for she had deliberately enticed Charles to the *Schloss* with the sole idea of becoming the wife of a fashionable English portrait-painter. She had been inspired to this end by the fact that a much disliked friend of hers had done the same thing a few months previously, and had shown the Baroness the way. Now she was made aware that there was something between him and her daughter, but she never flicked an eyelid.

She pulled herself together and still beamed as one complacent. 'Ver' *gut. Ebenso*,' she said. 'It is also *gut* to know he has the charming daughter. *So*.'

If Charles had gasped when he heard Julia break the news—it never lasted long with him— now he recovered and was himself once more. 'Weddings seem to run in our family for the moment,' he suggested.

79

'They do, don't they?' Daniel agreed.

The Baroness was busy making arrangements. 'Ve must have the vine for the vedding, *ja*, now,' she said, and led the way through the cluttered hall of the *Schloss* to the salon beyond it.

After lovely Wetherley the *Schloss* had what seemed like nightmare decorations. It was startlingly dissimilar to the fashionable hotels in the south of France from which Julia and Daniel had just come, for here was no Cluny and taffeta, nothing in the way of plaster cupids, and pale ribbons, orange and lemon trees and the eternal perfume of clove carnation and tuberose. If the hall had been a mess, the salon was a picture of a long-lost past, flustered by prominent furniture, too much velvet, too many bronze equestrians (there seemed to be dozens of them), yet from the window was a view that was entirely dazzling. The mountains had come much nearer. The hyacinth was veined in the startling silver of riotous waterfalls, the snow glittered with the white of sheer diamonds.

'The best vine,' said the Baroness impressively, and she bellowed for Karl to bring it.

Karl came rushing in. He was a stout little fellow who should never have worn Tyrolean dress. His little head and legs were out of proportion to the stout paunch emphasized by the distressing shorts that he wore. The best wine?

Ja, of course. Not that the Baroness would know the best from the worst, as he had long ago discovered when he had helped himself to bottle after bottle of the wine her father had laid down before her, and her grandfather before that, leaving his mistress just the everyday wine in abundance.

Charles looked at Daniel.

'You're fortunate,' he said recovering his poise, and having rounded a difficult corner rejoicing. 'How wise you were not to have a long engagement! It never pays. What did the village think of it all?'

'Mr. Lucas was a great help,' Julia told him, 'and Hoggie liked it.'

'I bet her tongue has wagged! Don't tell me, I know,' said Charles. 'This is going to be where the family lives happily ever after, isn't it?' and he rubbed his hands together, artistic hands small in contrast to his big body.

The Baroness glanced at him, and Julia saw the look. The Baroness was quite unlike anything she had expected, for Charles had lightly described her as a 'comic old bird', and as yet Julia could not recover from the shock of the first meeting. Perhaps Griselda had been the greater surprise, but Julia knew that she already liked her, and realized that even if she did become her stepmother she would act the part of a sister.

Never had she thought of the possibility of

Charles remarrying. The ground on which she stood, she had thought so securely, trembled with the amazement. Psychologically she knew that she was horribly shocked, and ashamed of it because she did so want his happiness.

She put out her hand and touched Daniel's arm, knowing that the events of today had brought them a great deal closer. Until this moment she supposed Charles had been something of a ghost standing between them for probably she loved him too much. Now everything was coming into the proper perspective; the man she loved with all her heart was Daniel, the second best was Charles.

The Baroness was busily proposing toasts. She loved her portrait, she insisted, and the thought of her daughter's marriage to so great a painter fascinated her.

'I did t'ink,' she said, warming with the wine Karl had produced, 'that he lose the 'eart to me. It 'appens much,' and she giggled like a girl. 'It is my affliction, *ja*. *Mein Gott*, the men that loves me! *Mein Gott*!'

'Naturally,' said Charles, who in the new mood could afford to be forgiving, and only hoped she would not cook up something else on him.

'More vine,' said the Baroness, 'then ve vill eat the *Mittagessen*.'

They drank and then went into the dining-room to eat an enormous meal in the old

Austrian style, the Baroness belching incongruously, for she delighted in the fact that she was the most natural woman in the world. She told highly coloured stories of her own conquests, of her sporting activities, the prizes she had won; she told of the night when a German prince had suggested an assignation, and she had defied him, tearing down the bedroom curtains and assaulting him with them. Griselda and Charles sat hand in hand well used to this, but Julia, growing somewhat embarrassed, wondered what Daniel thought of it.

She hoped that he liked Charles but could not be sure, and anyway the rest of the scene might be more than a trifle jarring. Long into the hot afternoon they sat in the atrocious room over the food, until the smell of pigeon pie, *Apfelstrudel*, and herring salad made the place almost unpleasant.

Then the two of them rose to leave.

'So soon?' gasped the Baroness.

'We have to get back,' said Daniel quietly, 'this is just a fleeting visit for we are flying home to England almost immediately, I am afraid.'

Julia had no idea that he had intended returning so soon. She looked at him dismayed by the news, for they had only just arrived and Charles was here. The whole day had been too much for her. Daniel turned and smiled to her. Suddenly she knew that he had realized what had happened. That she was a little disappointed, that the thought of her father's remarriage was something of a strain however well she accepted it, and that she was tired. He knew her better than she had thought possible. She smiled back at him and put out her hand, and he took it gently as one accepts flowers.

'Well, I shall be returning pretty soon now,' said Charles, 'married and all, what a party we'll be giving! That'll shake the Weald. By the by you had better break the news to Hoggie for me, Julie. Hoggie'll have forty fits. I have a hunch that "Him" will disapprove.'

He ought to tell Hoggie himself, she thought, and even as she realized it knew that a month ago she would have excused him, laughed at his boyishness. Now she was just a little impatient with it. But she said, 'I'll tell her.'

'Good girl!'

'I hope Griselda won't find country life awfully dull. It's simple in the Weald; nothing much ever happens, and it can be quite boring, does she know?'

'I was at school in England, and that was simple too.' She laughed as she said it. 'Nothing ever happened at school. My goodness! Those Sunday walks, and also I met your rice pudding. That is not exciting.'

'I'm afraid you'll have to put up with Hoggie's cooking. One day good, another bad, but when she is good her savoury pie is a gem.'

Charles chimed in at that. He was growing a little tired of *Apfelstrudel*. 'Ah, yes,' he agreed, 'I'd have you all know that Hoggie's savoury pie *is* something.'

They moved to the waiting car and got into it. Looking back from the window at the ill-matched trio who stood on the lawn before the *Schloss*, she thought, 'Either I or the Baroness is mad and I can't believe it is me!'

'Good-bye, good-bye,' they called.

'*Auf Wiedersehen*,' from the Baroness, and then in one of her brighter spurts of the English idiom, 'Bottoms up!'

As the car moved down the drive with the strongly acrid scent of the fir trees and out into the road beyond, they saw the valley lying beneath them bathed in the heat haze. Daniel took her hand. He looked into her eyes, and then she saw that he was bubbling with laughter, for the whole day had struck him as being in one way hilariously funny.

'It was like something out of a book,' he said.

'The woman's mad.'

'Of course she is. But the girl's a pet, and your father's a dear.' Then gently, 'You're not worrying about his marrying, are you? He has a right to his own happiness, you know.'

'Of course I'm not worried.'

'I didn't want you to be, but I felt it was something of a shock. Had to be that way.'

'A little bit,' she confessed.

85

He put his arms about her, and drew her to
him, then he said, 'Darling, I think this is where
our marriage really begins.'

He was right.

PART TWO

CHAPTER SIX

THEY did not return as soon as Daniel had suggested for there was some difficulty in getting a plane. In a way Julia was not disturbed, she would rather stay a little longer, she said, though Daniel insisted it must not be too long. The world had turned topsy-turvy seeing that it contained a future stepmother, though this new knowledge seemed to bring her far closer to her husband, and make the future clearer.

That night in the charming bedroom with the fir forest just below the window, he had drawn her into his arms, nuzzling her throat with his mouth and comforting her. If she cried a little, it was not for disappointment over her father, but for love of him.

They had come early to their room for the extraordinary day at the *Schloss* had been exhausting. She liked Griselda. No one must ever think that she didn't, for it would not be true. It was just that everything had changed so much and in a way that she had never contemplated, in a way which made her feel insecure in her home life, yet far more secure in her married one. It was hard to explain.

'But why didn't Charles write and tell me all about it?' she asked her husband, then a little sadly, 'I suppose if I told the truth I'd admit that he always puts off till tomorrow what he could do today.'

'And in that lies the rub.'

'Perhaps, but whatever it is I do love him. I wonder if Griselda cares for him as much as I do? In a different way I suppose,' she went on, 'and I imagine just as much. All people love or hate Charles, it's funny, isn't it?'

'I can imagine that,' Daniel had thought that Charles was immensely likeable, big and clumsy, gay enough and happy enough, but a little of him would probably go a long way. He put his arms around her. 'Don't fret about any of this, for we have one another, darling,' he said, 'it is the way life plans for us to grow away from our parents and love others. That is why you love me now, and perhaps why I love you.'

'I'm so lucky in having met you.'

It was curious that after the shock of today, and the bewildering dizziness of her changed world, tonight should be so happy with her husband. She fell asleep in his arms, curled against him, for all the time she was thinking of the portrait of a girl in riding clothes with her head flung back, against the background of an autumnal wood. She was remembering that once Theresa had been the most beautiful girl that he had ever seen, possibly the most attractive girl, also. She wished she knew more about her. She wished that she dare ask. The ghost of a girl who had once been everything to him and who now was merely a shadow, would not let her be.

I'm jealous, she thought, then she knew that was not so. It was far more that her whole life had been a life in which there were no secrets, and she hated living with a mysterious something that she did not understand. She and Charles had told each other everything, yet on second thoughts that was no longer true. He had not told her of his engagement.

Life was desperately perplexing.

They telephoned Charles to bring Griselda over to lunch next day. It was a mercy that the Baroness had one of her migraine headaches and had to refuse, for it meant that the four of them could be together, in a far better setting than the *Schloss*. Charles and Griselda drove over in the ancient open tourer on which the Baroness flew her own standard for she had been very taken with this idea when visiting England. To travel like royalty gave her a delicious sense of power and in Austria there was nobody to say her nay.

The lunch went well. Charles was in one of his gayest moods, Griselda had recognized Julia as a friend and they chattered amiably together. Charles realized that Julia had changed very much; he could not recover from his surprise at her expensive frocks, the shimmer of pearls at her throat and the exquisite way her hair was cut. She had always been elfish but now this was emphasized. She's a lot too young for Daniel, he thought, and then, that fellow looks as if he had had a secret past! He wondered if he was jealous of his own son-in-law—an absurd idea!; maybe he was.

At lunch, he learnt more about Daniel, Julia telling him glowingly of Eton and Worcester and of the Bar.

'He's a pilot too, Charles,' she told him.

Charles silenced the remark he would have made for he had a considerable dislike of anything that flew. 'Fine,' he said.

When they had done the day seemed cooler, for a slight breeze had got up and Griselda suggested a walk across the field below the window to the far forest where she understood there were some very special trees. Daniel offered to take her and in the end the four of them went.

Before they had gone very far Charles suggested that he and Julia should sit down on the grass amongst the foxgloves, and wait for the others to complete the trip and return.

'Oh yes,' said Julia, 'then we can talk.'

It was their first real talk together, the first one alone, and there should be so much to say. They sat on the turf verge edging the erratic little path which wound across three subsequent fields to the woods beyond. A cockeyed shrine, blown by the gusty gales of winter, stood a little

90

farther on, lurching incongruously. The backcloth of this hour was musical comedy. A sturdy farmer in shorts, with colourful braces and one of those ridiculous hats that had a shaving brush in it, walked past them. They talked.

'How about all this, Julie darling? He's a jolly fine chap, and you've done pretty well for yourself, I must say.'

She had meant to tell him everything and had waited for this moment believing that it would be the fulfilment of much, but now, when it actually came, she found that she was shrinking from him with a childlike shyness. She had never been like it with her father before. Maybe it was the picturesque setting, the foxgloves and the Canterbury bells, the old farmer with that ridiculous shaving brush in his hat, and the little shrines. When she thought again about it Charles did not really come into this, and it would be difficult to explain everything without involving Daniel. She must not do that for she was his wife.

In an instant Charles, unaware of the importance of the moment, had gone off on another tangent.

'What is Wetherley like?'

'You'll love it. It has a glorious line and such a beautiful fanlight over the door. A minstrels' gallery too, just everything. Daniel calls it a gracious lady and I think he is right. That is what Wetherley is.'

'And your sister-in-law?'

'Clare seems a great deal older than I am; she went to one of the famous public schools and I am sure she is awfully nice, but not—well, not our sort. Perhaps we are not moving on the same wavelength as you call it.'

He grinned at that.

'It's a well-known fact that sisters-in-law never get on well, but you and Griselda will be all right together because you are so much the same age. I suppose there are lots of servants at Wetherley so that you don't have to do a thing? No Hoggies?'

'There are three daily women who come and go, I understand. I saw the shadow of one of them, a thing called Cathie, just for a moment (dotty, I should have said). Mrs Marriner is the housekeeper. Charles, I don't like her.'

'That's a bad start, I must say.'

'She gives me the idea of being something of a Rosa Dartle, looks like it too. Apparently she likes working on her own, and she makes a good job of it, for the place is beautifully kept. When she first came Daniel had other servants but gradually she got rid of the lot.'

'Did she now? After the master, I suppose?'

'Oh no, no, not at all.'

But all this meant nothing. It just didn't count. Julia had meant to tell him about the letter that night, about the marriage lines which she had read in the car, and then about Theresa with her bewildering beauty and her supremacy; a ghost about the place, a ghost she could feel but never meet, a girl of whom she knew nothing; and the fact that Daniel would not talk.

Yet sitting here with the smell of countrified verdure, with the mountains in the distance and the shrines, she came to the decision that all this must be something between herself and Daniel. She had already travelled that far in marriage. They were each other's and they shared; they would share for the rest of their lives; so she told Charles nothing at all.

He did not notice it.

He was gaily and amusingly telling her of his own experiences. Last night, would you believe it, that wily old Baroness had cheated at Bridge! She always did it vaguely, glossing over it with casual unconcern, but last night it had been positively outrageous and she had won quite a lot from him. One thing was certain, Griselda would never grow up like her *Müttchen* (damn the old woman!), she had been too brow-beaten for that, and although he sympathized with the sort of early life she must have endured with such a mother, he was darned glad that she was not going to be of the same mould.

Anyway he had a cheque for a thousand pounds in his pocket, and that was something, wasn't it?

'That ought to set everything straight,' agreed

Julia, and she laughed.

'Griselda and I are going to get married very quietly, I could not stand a big wedding with the Baroness on the bust. You can imagine how she'd take it! I want you when you get back, dear, to tell Hoggie all about it. At no cost must she walk out on me, and I don't care if she says there's no fool like an old fool, that's bound to come.'

'I'll have a talk with Hoggie.'

Julia was still playing with the idea of trying to tell him about the anonymous letter which was her main worry. Perhaps she had been silly to let the conversation slip on to Hoggie's reactions to the marriage, but should have pursued it to its proper end. She tried to steel herself to bring back the subject, but somehow she never came to it and Charles was still chattering on.

'I tell you this'll give that silly village something to think about. I bet Mr. Lucas will have something to say, and the talk will shake the Weald. By the by, I believe that absurd old Baroness thought she was going to be the bride. You won't be able to believe it, darling, but she made passes at me! Only the other night when we got left together to play bezique—a gruesome game—she certainly made passes. If you want to know the truth it sent me into a cold sweat.'

'How utterly awful!'

'I thought I'd have to cut and run, the coward's way out of course, but better live to fight another day than continue when on the losing side. I hadn't dared tell her about Griselda—you did that for me.'

'I did?'

'Yes, when you arrived! The old bird hadn't a clue until you let it out. For a moment I nearly swooned, but she took it like a true blue, and never batted an eyelid. Today she tossed the cheque to me, at one in the morning it was, just after she had cheated me so disgracefully at Bridge, you really wouldn't have thought it, would you? But she is a remarkable woman.'

'I think she is mad.'

'Of course she is. Nearly shot me when I arrived, but the portrait will be shown in Vienna, and I hope to get other extravagant commissions from it. I rather think I'm in luck.' Perhaps he noticed the sadness in those grey-blue eyes of hers, the droop of her mouth, for he jerked himself back to her love story. 'You two met at Stratford?'

'Yes, in the theatre. Daniel had a spare ticket and was returning it. I'd tried to book and there wasn't a seat left, so he gave his to me.'

'Goodness! That's a pretty corny story, darling.'

'Oh no, Charles, it wasn't that one, truly it wasn't. We fell in love right away and got married. That's all.'

'Knowing nothing about him? Why, he might have done anything, he might have been an out-and-out cad. Darling, you *are* the most simple child!'

'I knew I loved him,' she said, and now she realized that welded her to Daniel. She could not confide in Charles because she felt that he would never understand it all, and she must face this alone, because that was the way it was working out.

'That's the idea,' said her father brightly, and went on to another subject. 'I shall paint a picture of you and Griselda together, she with her plaits down—I have a thing about those plaits of hers—your light eyes and her deeper ones. Might get it into Burlington House, if the old what-nots will pass it, but you know what *they* are! Anyway it would be a cert for the British Portrait Society. I could call it *Les Girls*—or not!'

'Darling Charles!'

No, after all she would tell him nothing. He had brought the conversation right back to the subject and still she shrank. Theresa was dead. If she had not received the anonymous letter that night she might not have exaggerated the position as perhaps she had done. Time would help her silence that exaggeration. Time would be her greatest help. With the whole of her future life beside Daniel before her, at all costs she must lay that ghost.

Charles was still talking. So much had happened and he was so ebulliently happy that he could not stop. Two nights previously they had all visited a night club in Innsbrück and he had adored it.

'All that slap-and-tickle stuff,' said he, 'you know what it is, and before we knew where we were the leader of the orchestra had stepped down and insisted that the Baroness should conduct the band. Up she went, Griselda and I blushing for shame, but we needn't have worried for she knocked hell out of that orchestra, and they gave her a gingerbread heart as a reward. You never saw anything like it. Having done that, out she stepped on to the floor with a fellow she said was an archduke (he looked like a road-sweeper to me) and they began to dance. What a woman!'

'You should have married her, Charles; think how it would have surprised Hoggie!'

'It would have surprised me a good deal more. Oh no, let her stay as she is. Let her open her purse strings, and she does that, for she can be generous when in the right mood. Griselda's *dot* is going to be something, we may even get a new roof on to the house with it, and the Lord only knows we need it. She is giving us a little house here in the corner of the grounds; she calls it *Das klein Schloss*, which of course it isn't at all. It's just a pre-fab of sorts, nice for week-ends. Little more.'

'Well, I think the Baroness is a far more suitable model for you than Mrs. Tanner from Sevenoaks who looked like a tired pork pie.'

Julia saw the others coming back and rose to meet them. Even as she did so she knew that she had not achieved her end. Now for the future she must face this alone. It doesn't matter, she thought.

★ ★ ★

A week later she and Daniel flew home.

Daniel had had a worrying letter. He was connected with several companies, which meant nothing to Julia who had never had anything to do with companies in her life. He sat on boards, and something had gone amiss with a certain Swedish concern, which demanded his presence at a board meeting in London.

'We'll come back here later, darling,' he said.

'In some ways it'll be nice to get home for England is so lovely at this time of year, but I've got to tell Hoggie about Charles's marriage, and that is going to be a job.'

'Hoggie struck me as being an old vixen.'

'Your Mrs. Marriner struck me much the same way.'

Daniel was packing a suitcase and he turned and looked at her. 'Mrs. Marriner has had the devil of a time, you know. She was in Holland during the war and actually saw her father shot.

She starved. That's why she eats so little now; she had become so accustomed to deprivation. Clare sits on lots of committees and charitable organizations, and she found Mrs. Marriner, for which I am very grateful, for she has done wonders for Wetherley.'

'I'm sure she has.' In a way Julia was half ashamed that she could not feel deeply sorry for the woman. Her slenderness, her sharp little hatchet of a face, and the eyes rather like those of some bird of prey, had not given the impression that she came from Holland.

'Is she Dutch?' she asked.

'I don't really know, but I don't think so. She is very hard worker and that is what matters to me.'

Julia felt that in some strange way he was silencing her, and she did not pursue the subject. She must never mention Theresa, and it would almost seem that she must be careful what she said about Mrs. Marriner. She had to be careful. With him the difficulty was that she never was aware of danger before she had touched it.

They caught the midday plane.

Charles and Griselda came to see them off, arriving in the car with the standard fluttering before it, but without the Baroness, who was indisposed again. She really should never eat duck but had done, and now was in a darkened room living on lemon juice.

The airport received the Baroness's car as though it carried a Hohenzollern before the war. In it Charles sat with a smirk, waving a friendly hand to saluting officials, and bouncing out on to the red carpet with the *sang froid* air of a genial Englishman who considers that the whole thing is one big hell of a joke! Griselda, wearing a curious combination of national and modern dress, for which her mother should have taken out a patent, walked beside him.

Instantly the airport was all alert.

The four of them met in a private waiting-room, a tardy attendant rushing in perspiring, and carrying a vase of flowers for the table. About the place was an air of disuse and stuffiness.

'Nobody could say we didn't do the thing in style!' announced Charles.

Somehow it hurt Julia that he should have adopted this fashion of the semi-national dress, a creamy coat with embroidered lapels over the shorts which his figure disgraced, and the *Lederhosen* of which he was so proud.

*   *   *

'I'm going up in the world,' he said. 'If Hoggie and 'Him' could have seen that they would have had a fit. When she gets over the shock, Julie, tell her that we shall sneak home for a quiet wedding there rather than have a

100

cathedral ceremony here. We'll be back soon.'

'I'll tell her everything.'

Julia could see the plane beyond the window, a smaller one than she had previously travelled in. Although in one way she wanted to be up and away from this pantomime exhibition, in another the dignity of Wetherley might become alarming. She must not think of it. Griselda spoke to her quietly.

'I'll love Kent, Julie; I know I shall.'

'It'll be cold after summer in this part of the world.'

'We ski here when winter comes. We get fearful snowstorms and it can be quite awful.'

'In Kent the wind comes over the sea and that can be pretty stinging. All the same Charles and I have always loved it.'

An official came to the door with every sign of deep respect, and announced that it was time they embarked.

Charles gulped down a last drink; Griselda kissed Julia with real affection, and they went out of the private room. They had hardly moved away before the same perspiring attendant bolted in to retrieve the vase of flowers which had been merely a temporary measure and now were due elsewhere.

They walked across the tarmac, parting at the barrier; Julia and Daniel going on, waved back to the two still waiting. Charles was waving the Tyrolean hat which had given him such qualms, and there was real triumph in his eyes. Julia climbed up the gangway into the little plane and saw the friendly stewardess waiting for her and she conducted her to a seat.

'After all, it's nice to be going home, Daniel.'

'Nice that Wetherley is home to you. Always think of it that way.'

'I do.'

Guessing what she thought, he said, 'Mrs Marriner won't worry you, and Clare lives in the Dower House on the other side of the park, nothing need worry you.'

'Of course not,' but all the time she knew that everything was going to be entirely different from anything she had ever known before in the happy-go-lucky cottage with Hoggie. Butterflies stirred within her. There was a certain whimsical fear, a premonition of disaster, but she reassured herself that she could conquer it.

They took off and almost at once she realized that this was going to be a far more difficult flight. The plane kept banking on the left wing, swerving as it turned in a very alarming way. The day, which had been radiantly fair on the ground, was not good for flying, and almost at once she felt sick. There had been a few unpleasant air pockets, and all the time there came that urgent prayer within her that the plane would travel more smoothly. It got better for a time, and she confessed how horribly ill she had felt; then after a few minutes' smoother flying they plunged down again and this time she was sick. The stewardess came to her aid and promised her there was nothing really wrong, and it would be much better when they left the mountains behind them, which would not be long. But even as she said it the plane dropped again and Julia's body rebelled.

Later, when it did get better as the stewardess had promised, Julia felt so limp that she could not even be grateful. Mercifully she dozed a little, and woke only when Daniel laid a comforting hand on her icy one. They were touching down at London airport, and never had she felt more relieved.

Her immediate desire was to leave the plane behind her and step out into the beautiful freedom of the clear evening. The air was a joy. Her head still ached but she was not as weak as she would have expected to be. They went to the Customs building, then on to Daniel's waiting car, turned out of the gates, and took the road towards Slough.

'You'll feel better quite soon, Julie, for we're going home.'

'Will Clare be there?'

'Not tonight. This, the first night, we'll be together, and I suggest that you go straight to bed and let Mrs. Marriner bring you some food later.'

'I—I feel so awfully ashamed.'

'I don't see why. It happens to all of us at

103

some time or another, and that was a pretty nasty flight. I felt quite queasy myself at times.'

She was grateful for the pleasant chilliness of the evening in England. The bluebells had come. A may tree showed its first crystal white against a sky that was palely blue in contrast, yet rosying in the west. They turned in at the gates of Wetherley, with the evening closing in, and she saw the pool like milk before the house, the shadow of a hawthorn bush the only dark smudge upon its white surface.

As they moved together up the steps the door opened, and there was Mrs. Marriner, waiting for them. She looked tight-lipped even though she smiled, and her hands were folded on her stomach as before, her face very pale.

'Welcome home,' she said.

'Madam was ill in the plane—it was horribly bumpy—and she is going straight to bed,' Daniel explained.

'Dinner shall go up to her, sir,' and Mrs. Marriner stood back for them.

They went across the hall with here and there a light already burning, shaded in red velvet and fringed with dark gold. Julia went along the corridor to the room which in some way was already home, Henry, the chauffeur, following with the cases and Mrs. Marriner behind him.

'If you take a bath, madam, I'll unpack. It'll all be ready by the time you are,' she said gently.

The woman was good at her work, one had to

admit that. Julia went limply into the bath already run for her and with *eau de Cologne* perfume dropped into it. Mrs. Marriner would not have made the mistake of using lily of the valley, or lilac or rose, for someone who felt ill. It was a joy to slip out of her clothes and into the water, Julia decided, her body firm like a child's with not an ounce of fat on it, her skin like marble. The sweet-smelling water revived her, and she did not hurry but came out of the bath only when it had refreshed her. She drew on a French nightdress, one of Daniel's gifts to her, and a silk dressing-gown sprayed with pink roses in shadow quilting.

After all, she would want food.

She had only just got into the bed when Mrs. Marriner wheeled in a trolley. 'I think, madam, it would be wise to eat simply,' she said, 'which is why I did not bring up the same meal as is being served downstairs.'

Asparagus lay in a silver dish; there was cold chicken and a young fresh salad that was delicious. There was fruit and a coffee percolator being kept hot over a tiny jet flame. Julia thought of Hoggie, whose be-all and end-all in emergencies was the boiled egg, poached if it was a real crisis, otherwise boiled. 'Eggs is good,' Hoggie insisted. 'Nobody can do better than eggs. "Him" says there's downright life in 'em.'

Tomorrow Julie would have to tell Hoggie

about Griselda, and that was going to be difficult. She refused to think of it now, but ate the food slowly and lay back afterwards with the coffee, and was annoyed that she should ask herself: Did Theresa sleep in this room? Did she wake to look out at the view over the Hog's Back? Did she hold Daniel's hand here? Kiss him? Love him? She was intensely curious. She wanted to know about Theresa, what sort of a person she had been, how the two of them had met and if they were very much in love.

Did the writer of the anonymous letter know about Theresa? But of course she must have done. A woman! Long ago she had convinced herself that it must have been a woman, and somewhere in the world there was someone, close up against Julie's own life, who knew everything that she was doing and could perhaps even hear what she said.

Apprehension came to her.

The ghost of Theresa was that of a woman who was dead, but there was a living person left who could write letters, and who knew things about her.

The door opened. She had been thinking so vividly of ghosts, two of them, that she was almost surprised to see Daniel coming in. He knows all the answers, she thought. If only she could draw him into her arms and say, 'Tell me everything about Theresa, and what she meant to you, and what she still means to you?' it would be such a help. But she could not do it.

'Hello darling! Better?'

'Much better. A bath can be such a joy, and then the loveliest meal.'

'Mrs. Marriner does this sort of thing rather well. May I help myself to some of your coffee?'

'Of course.' He seemed to be relaxed, and in this mood she wondered if there were not questions that she could ask him, reasoned with herself for a moment and during that time he started to talk of Wetherley. 'I want you to know, darling, that if there is anything you want altered you have only got to say so. Rearrange any of the rooms the way you wish, for the ready-made home may not be what you like.'

'I wouldn't want to alter anything,' she said.

'There's the new rock garden I want to build. I have the plans. There is a spring at hand and we could turn it into a little stream running through it, with rustic bridges over it. We'll plan it together.'

'It'll be lovely.'

He said almost nostalgically: 'I have so wanted someone to share this place with me. Clare was never the right sort; we have never seen eye to eye. She means well, but we are not alike. I was always the nomad of the three of us. She and my brother were cut to pattern, but I was different. Everything I did was not what they would have done. Now I've got someone to share Wetherley with me,' and there was a plaintive tone in his voice.

Julia reached out her hand and took his. Very gently she said, 'Didn't Theresa share it?'

They looked into each other's eyes and she had the feeling that he had receded from her. He said nothing. If he had said one single word it could have been such a help, but there was only the silence of his cold disapproval. After what seemed to be for ever, he spoke in a changed voice.

'It's strange, I suppose, but I don't want to talk about any of that. It's all over and done with, gone for ever, and I don't want to remember it.' He went over to the window, and taking out his cigarette-case from his pocket selected a cigarette and lit it with a shaky hand. A night bird squawked in the trees, and then Julia knew that she was going to cry.

★　　　★　　　★

She drove over to see Hoggie next day.

Daniel took her in the little car which they used for shopping in Guildford or Aldershot. As they neared the Weald and the familiar places came into sight, Julia realized that it seemed she had been away for an eternity. The apples had finished blossoming; the crown imperials had died in the vicarage garden, and the lupins were in flower, boldly extravagant, in blue and pink and deep purple.

108

They stopped outside the cottage and as the noise of the engine ceased they heard the sound of Hoggie singing as was her wont.

> Rock of Ages cleft for me,
> Let me hide myself in Thee.

'That choice means it is one of her good days,' whispered Julia. 'It would have been a very different story if she had been singing 'Be Thou my Guardian and my Guide'. That always means businesss.'

Hoggie was of Baptist persuasion, 'Him' was nothing at all. She was interested in revivalist meetings, which maddened Charles. How he hated 'Rock of Ages'! 'Something to do with Cheddar Gorge,' he said once, 'and why didn't Cheddar Gorge keep it, I'd like to know?'

Julia went up the crazy path that she had laid herself, now well aware of the unfortunate crevices growing wider with every winter storm. She was back in her old home, grey slacks, light cashmere jumper and all. Her hair was loose in the wind, the thick cap of hair like a child's. Perhaps she had never been intended for the grand lady type. She went into the living-room. Hoggie was turning out the side cupboard by the ingle, where Charles kept all his rough sketches, which he never allowed to be moved if he could help it; but now Hoggie had got at them.

109

She sat back on her stout haunches. 'So it's you, Miss Julie? Well I never! You've got back, have you? My, but you look peaky; too much rich food! Nothing like a good boiled egg, I always says. "Him" thinks that too.' She clicked her false teeth defiantly, which she always did when emphasizing a point. Did you see your dad?'

'I did indeed. He'll be back soon.' Julia plunged wildly into the truth, knowing that if she did not tell Hoggie now she would never be able to do it. 'He's getting married.'

'What did you say, Miss Julie?'

'He's marrying again.'

'My goodness! I do hope as how she's suitable.'

'She's my age and I like her awfully.'

'YOUR age?' Horror had come into Hoggie's peering eyes. 'But he's old, Miss Julie. What's more, he's old enough to know better. It would never do for him to marry some little bit like that! A flibbertigibbet, I dare reckon.'

'No, she isn't. I think she's lovely.'

'Oh!' There was a long pause, with Hoggie growing more and more like the Rock of Ages herself, then she spoke again. 'I thought there was something funny about him staying out there all this time, and what's more "Him" said so, too.' She clicked her teeth again. 'Don't let him do nothink so silly, Miss Julia. He knows nothink about her and he'll only live to regret it,

110

I'm sure.'

'What was that you said?'

'Don't let him do it, Miss Julia. He's getting on. He'll find it downright hard going keeping up with somebody young. He hadn't ought to try it on.'

'I've never thought of him as being old.'

'But he IS old, everybody knows he's old, and love isn't no good when you're that age.'

Julia stood there in the familiar room where soon Griselda would reign as mistress, and she said, 'We can't interfere, Hoggie, and whatever you say I like her and think she's nice.'

'It won't work out, Miss Julie. I promise you that one.'

Julia walked past her into the studio and she drew back the linen sheet which protected the picture on the easel. Mrs. Tanner, with her tired pork-pie face, looked now to be tragically unfinished, and Julia wondered if Charles would ever bring himself to add those difficult final touches. There had been only two portraits so far which had reached this stage and still were undone. That horrid little boy with the marmalade-coloured hair and freckles, and Charles had only agreed to paint him when he had had one too many in 'The Pride of the Weald.' Two sittings had left him in despair, but he had worked on and then had finally had to give up the ghost. The other had been of that poor young girl who had been killed in a car accident and whose canvas was turned to the wall for ever. Charles felt bad about that to this day. Was Mrs. Tanner going to be another one of them?

The whole of their lives had changed when Charles had set off to Innsbrück, and Julia had gone to Stratford-on-Avon. Or had it been the night before her marriage when she had found the letter which was unsigned lying on the mat?

She replaced the dust sheet over the canvas and returned to the living-room. Hoggie was sweeping up and clicking her teeth in a rage. Just before Julia left she came to the door with her, the scent of wallflowers and narcissi blowing into the house.

'I do think as how you ought to stop your dad, Miss Julia! This'll never work out. A kid like that, and her an Australian too! Tst! Tst! Tst!'

'Oh, it'll be all right.'

Privately she thought that Charles would be contented enough, but she disliked the faint underlying doubt which disturbed her. He has *got* to be happy, she told herself.

★   ★   ★

It was morning at Wetherley.

She and Daniel walked across the park to visit Clare and take her the current issues of the *Tatler* and the *Queen*, apparently a routine duty. The hot day was coming up, but at this hour it

112

was not too irksome, with the river, already low for it had been a dry spring, running one side of the path, and the forget-me-nots blue across the bank. Until today Daniel had always seemed much older than Julia was, but as they walked now she got the feeling that he was younger; her age; part of her. She had the happy feeling that they belonged, and perhaps at no time since her marriage had she felt so tranquil with him. Her hair was tossed back in the breeze, her cotton frock cut low and short, and about her the *gamine* joy of being alive.

'Oh, I am so happy,' she cried.

'I love you, Julie, and you love me. I suppose I loved you from that very first moment when I saw you turning away so disappointedly from the box office at Stratford. I knew I loved you.'

'Charles said that was the corny approach.'

'It wasn't an approach at all, and not one bit corny. It was the only thing I could do.'

'Do I come up to expectations, Daniel?'

'In every way. So sweet! So young! So lovely! I daren't ask you if I come up to expectations for maybe I am a funny kind of a fellow. One day we'll know one another better, but for now'— and he laughed—'we'll do.'

'That's a promise, Daniel?'

She had adored Charles—still did—but Daniel was different because she was his wife. In the brilliant sunshine of the fetid hot May morning no ghost lurked with the deer among

113

the trees. No memory pierced her confidence and confused her. She raced him across the grass where he and his brother had raced as children, his brother always winning. His brother is dead, she thought, brought up abruptly by the thought of that loss.

'You have such long legs,' she panted, 'you ought to give me a start. It's cheating if you don't.'

'But you have half my years, or almost. That's cheating on your side, isn't it?'

'Very well, we won't race.'

They walked arm in arm to the house which Daniel told her used to be called Apple Trees but which Clare had changed to the Dower House. She had ordered all the apple trees to be cut down, which made him sad, for even if they were old and their fruiting pock-marked, their blossom was a surge of pearl beauty in the spring, The house which came into sight was dull and small, Julia thought, squat in build, and slate-roofed, the slates gathering a certain iridescence in the bright sunlight.

Daniel walked on ahead, opening the door, Julia following him. It was an interior which had no personality, and she recognized the lack immediately. Daniel called to his sister, then went into the sitting-room, a drab place, paper and chintzes selected without any thought of their relationship, and a clutter of ornaments which were dissociated each from the others.

114

Clare was sitting at a small escritoire in the window, apparently dealing with bills judging by the litter of headed papers which she had flung down on to the floor beside her.

'I never thought you would be here so early,' she said.

'It was such a lovely morning.'

'Yes, of course, but hot, and you know what too much sun does to you, Daniel. You've got no hat.' Then she turned to Julia. 'I'm afraid this house is very small after Wetherley, but we can't all be rich. It's nice to see you here.'

'It's a nice house.'

'Go over it as you wish, anywhere you like, then Daniel and I can have a chat. It's about these wretched accounts again, Daniel; I never know exactly what happens but things seem to be in a jam again and I—I hate doing it, but I shall have to ask for a small loan.'

'You're always asking for loans, Clare, and most of them are not small.'

'I know. This shall be the last time. Come and have a look at the books, then you'll see what has happened.'

He walked over to the littered escritoire, and realizing that she was not wanted Julia slipped out of the room. At the far end of the hall a daily woman was polishing; she was a bulky person who waddled about in a limp and tatty overall, her swollen feet thrust into bedroom slippers with distressed rabbit fur worn thin at the sides.

Julia went out through the side door, across a cobbled, weed-ridden yard, with a broken-down coal-shed to one side and a soft-water pump, little and dumpy, in the corner. Now she could see the raw stumps of the sawn apple trees about the house in a strange sort of Druids' circle of their own. They stood ominously, some already rotting from last winter's rain, others stocky, defiant, rather horrid-looking, she thought. The garden was full of the spring abundance of wallflowers, narcissi, primulas and budding lupins; going into the walled back garden she saw horseradish, mint, cabbages and the rising new potatoes, but all of them seemed to be subdued by the surround of these old stumps which once had given the name to the house.

In a way Julia felt angry with Clare for having cut down such beauty. She rebelled against it for surely they had done no harm, and, as Daniel had said, they had been unbelievably attractive when in blossom. They reminded her today of old decayed teeth in some unpleasantly ancient mouth, teeth that at life's beginning had been little pearls.

Clare came to her after a time, and by her manner Julia gathered that the talk with Daniel had not been propitious, though Clare actually said nothing.

'You live in the Weald?' she asked. 'Your father has a studio there, hasn't he?'

'Yes. Charles is really quite a famous artist.

116

One day you must come and see his pictures.'

'Once I saw the house, I believe.'

'You saw it? Why didn't you come in?'

Clare was entirely calm. She had a non-committal way of speaking which was difficult to pierce. 'It was late, I suppose. I remember someone mentioned your father and pointed out the house to me. I thought it charming, but wondered how he managed to paint there seeing it was so small.'

'There is a big studio at the back; once it was an old barn and Charles vows that it still smells of hops. He bought the house for that; the barn, I mean, not the smell of hops.'

'I see.'

They walked across the cobbled yard, and Clare referred to the pigsties she wanted put up. Money was close. George, her late husband, had left so little, and although Daniel was good to her she wanted to earn for herself. They came round to the front of the house again, and if it had grown rather wild, it had a singular disorderly beauty of its own. The jagged old stumps of trees pursued them wherever they went.

The daily woman came out to hang tea towels to dry on the line, and they stopped to speak to her.

'It's such a lovely day,' said Julia. 'When May IS nice it is the best month of the whole year, isn't it?'

'Ah!' said the woman. 'But that dangerous! My old man died in May; summer pneumonia they said, but it wasn't the summer, it was May, and May plays tricks, it do.'

'Yes.' There was little else that one could say.

They went on and into the house, pleasingly cool after the burning heat in the garden. Clare talked, but Julia got the impression that what she said was insincere; she always kept her personality shrouded, and in some ways was like Daniel in that. Wetherley was friendly and welcoming; the Dower House was not. Clare said that she only had the one woman in and she came for two hours a day; Clare spent the rest of her time entirely alone. Daniel had explained that she liked living alone, and had always refused to have anybody living in, so that daily women came and went. At Wetherley they did much the same thing, for Mrs. Marriner was the only resident. Mrs. Bentley, the wife of a young sailor now stationed in Malta, came in; Cathie Hawkes, who was not quite 'the thing', and had never been 'the thing', but was a good worker; and Rita Forbes, widowed by an accident in the harvest field, and glad to pick up a little extra.

Julia and Daniel walked back across the park, which was now swelteringly hot, for the temperature was soaring.

'You should have brought a hat,' she said. 'Clare noticed it, too.'

'Clare would! I hate the things. Oh, I know

118

the sun upsets me easily, but I'm all right.' He turned to the subject that was worrying him. 'I can't think how Clare always gets so short of money. She continually wants something by which she can earn, then drops the idea the moment I get it for her. In the far shed the incubator is rotting its guts out. Two years ago it was tomato houses; they are idle now. She says there's nothing in them, which is only too true. Before that it was chickens. Now she wants to take up pigs.'

'Was she left with nothing?'

'George left her a little, about seven hundred a year, I suppose. She lives rent free, but she has always been the restless kind. Her trouble has been she could never settle. It started at school, went with her to Girton, then she ran away with George.'

'Was he nice?'

'I think so, but I hardly knew him and she never talks about him. Clare likes to go her own way. She has a horde of old school-friends and goes round staying with them. I must say none of them come to stay with her, and that is just that.' He paused. 'In a way she nurses a sickly resentment that Wetherley goes down in the male line. I don't know why, seeing that most houses do this; she wanted it.'

'You help her?'

'Help her?' He lifted his dark eyes to heaven in mock despair. 'You can't imagine what Clare has had and what she still hopes to get. Maybe I'm mean. I told you we never saw eye to eye, and maybe that is the root of the trouble.'

He mopped his brow with a Paisley handkerchief. Julia realized that he found Clare tiresome; she thought her so herself, yet was sorry for her if she was hard-up. Daniel did not appreciate how difficult shortage of money could be.

They crossed the exposed patch of park to the house, the sun beating down, and the heat seeming to rise up at one and the same moment. Even Julia felt it.

'It's making my head ache,' Daniel said, and turning to look at him she saw that he had flushed. 'It's a heat that creeps all over me.'

'Get a shower before lunch,' she suggested.

He said that he would, yet when they got indoors, he sagged down wearily into a chair like a tired man, not sleeping, yet certainly not awake. An hour later he was sick and the pain in his head had become an insistent fire that burnt him up. After that he seemed to pass into periods of alarming uncertainty as though he was not quite aware of what was happening or where he was, and the village doctor—Dr. Middleton—came in. He was a middle-aged man, greyed yet genial, kindly and considerate.

'It's the sun again, and what is more he is always doing it. He never should play tricks with it, but he will do this.'

Through the long afternoon Daniel was aware of cool hands touching him, and a cold bandage being changed on his head. He fell asleep still burningly hot, and he woke after what appeared to be hours of pain, shuddering and dreadfully cold. Instantly the kind hands laid a blanket over him and he heard her voice speaking with that tender reassurance.

He had never thought that she would be so considerately gentle, or so understanding of his needs even before he himself realized them. He tried to kiss her hand, and she laid her face beside his on the pillow.

'You'll be better soon now. It's getting better already, just as Dr. Middleton said it would. You mustn't worry.'

He trusted her.

Until this moment he had not understood that he could turn to her, for she had seemed too young, but now he knew how desperately he wanted her. The warmth of the blanket helped his disturbed body and gave him a sense of well-being which he had lost *pro tem*.

He dozed for a while and woke much restored, to find Julia, still dressed, curled up asleep like a small child against him. She had worn herself out on his behalf. He looked at her, the silk frock now crumpled, and he saw the room cluttered with numerous things she had prepared for him; a bowl of water, a Thermos of iced lemon, a fan whirling on the far table, and another blanket in readiness in case the feeling of cold returned. Everywhere that he looked he saw the signs of her pathetic anxiety for him. He lay very still. He loved her, and was ashamed that he could not tell her so more vehemently. If only he could tell her everything, but there was too much! And half the trouble was that other people's secrets were knotted into it, so that he dare not start.

Julia turned in her sleep and instinctively clung to him.

*   *   *

Daniel was ill for quite a few days and weak from the pain, during which time the hot weather broke, and a chilly rainy June was born. The Hog's Back was blotted out and even the park grew dim. This was when the cable arrived from Charles.

The portrait of the Baroness being finally varnished and on show in Vienna, where it had been generously received, he and Griselda were getting married and coming home.

Tell Hoggie to prepare for us, he cabled.

Julia read it with apprehension. It had arrived during a late breakfast on the terrace.

'Hoggie is going to hate this,' she said.

'Of course, but she'll have to put up with it'— Daniel was quite calm—'and you do want your father back, don't you, darling? I'm not quite

122

enough alone. You were always too fond of him; I know that.'

'I want both of you, but you first,' she said, and realized that it sounded limp, rather silly, not deep down in her heart as she really meant it.

In truth Charles had had to rush his wedding. At the last moment the Baroness turned nasty, went away on a hunting expedition, and he took advantage of her absence to get married. Her surprise and fury would be rather funny when she got back, he thought, as the night train sped him across Europe home with his bride.

They got home unexpectedly—he had not had time to warn Julia any more—and on a wet June evening. He thought that the house looked very pretty as the taxi drew up at the gate, but he hated the expense of hiring it all the way from Sevenoaks. They cost the earth these days.

He could see that Hoggie had had the good sense to light a fire, for the pastel blue smoke curled up from the chimney against the darkness of June-time trees. They went up the path hand in hand, the drenched flowers just lifting their heads again, for the rain had ceased and a fitful sun was beginning to come out over the Weald. The smell of the moist earth was sweet, and he liked the sound of the birds singing. England was better than Austria, even if it did rain.

Hoggie was singing 'Be Thou my Guardian

123

and my Guide,' which told Charles exactly where he was, and he groaned a little! As he opened the door gaiety inspired him, and impulse egged him on.

'I must carry you over the threshold, my darling. We always do. It's an old English custom coming from Spain,' and he swung Griselda up into his arms.

He strode into the house with her; she seemed to be a trifle heavy, or maybe he was a little tired, but it had been a difficult journey and he only hoped that he did not wobble with her. He kissed her boisterously before he put her down, and became aware of somebody standing there and staring at him across the room. Small and tubby, with that absurdly small head, the narrow shoulders and the hips like the buttresses of some capacious bridge. It was Hoggie.

'So, YOU'VE come home, have you?' she said.

CHAPTER SEVEN

NEXT day, bright and early, Daniel brought Julia over in the car. She had been in ecstasy that her father was home again, delighted to think that Griselda would be now established, and she rushed into the house on one of those glowing summer mornings when the sun of today tries to make amends for the rains of yester-eve. Julia ran up the garden path with the joyous feeling that this was the day. Hoggie met her at the door.

'She didn't eat no breakfast,' said Hoggie, and her face was gloom personified. 'Just a bit of toast. Said she never had nothing but toast. And coffee. I always thinks there's something a bit fooney about people what only drinks coffee.'

'Continental breakfast,' said Julia gaily.

Hoggie stared at her with the look of one who has no idea what she is talking about, then she said, 'WELL, it all sounds a bit fooney to me,' and sniffed. Hoggie could make a wonderful lot of a sniff.

By contrast Charles was in convivial good spirits and came in from his studio.

'You must both come over and have lunch with us; we've come to fetch you,' Julia said.

'That'll suit me fine.' He dropped his voice. 'There's been a spot of bother here and the whole house is "Be Thou my Guardian and my Guide". Hoggie doesn't approve of Griselda not wanting our sort of breakfast, and it is hardly joyous. Then the Baroness has sent me a disgusting cable. We slipped out and got married whilst she was off on a hunting expedition. It seemed to be the right opportunity and there was no reason for her to be annoyed. But she *is* annoyed. What a woman!'

'Well, she can't get at you here.'

'I know; that's something. Take us over in your car, let's see Wetherley, and the pool before the house, the minstrels' gallery, and the lot. You haven't got a ghost to go with it all, have you?'

She said 'No' almost sharply, for there *was* a ghost at Wetherley, the ghost of the first wife, something Julia had been aware of from the very beginning, something that she could not escape.

Griselda had hardly finished her unpacking, and upstairs the place was a shambles. The house was small, the space constricted, and after the *Schloss* the girl was finding it difficult. Hers was not a tidy nature. In Austria there had been people to tidy up after her, and although she did not realize it, Hoggie was not likely to do anything for her here. When they had prepared to start for Wetherley Hoggie had gone quiet, which was usually a good sign and the prelude to 'Rock of Ages'.

'We're taking Charles and Griselda back to have lunch with us,' Julia told her, going into the kitchen in a friendly way and trying to coax her.

Across the table Hoggie glared at her. 'And me with a queen's pudding in the oven and all!'

'You can give it to them for supper tonight.'

Hoggie clicked her false teeth together. One of her favourite habits was making an absurd sort of tin music with her false teeth, and she did

126

it more than ever when she was angry. 'She's nothink but a kid, she is! What's more she don't know nothink and ought never to have married. I don't know what the world's coming to, I don't, and him carrying her over the threshold, and all that there. "Him" said it showed they was dotty, and that's what it is, if you ask me.'

'She'll learn what to do in time.'

'Oh well, I shouldn't worry. All today's bothers usually come out in tomorrow's wash,' Julia told her.

'That what you thinks, and this time it don't work. This lot'll want a downright good boil to get it out. "Him," says so, and he knows. It's wonderful what "Him" knows about life.'

Julia left her at that. Personally she would never have thought that 'Him' was particularly knowledgeable; he was a short, stocky man with putty-coloured cotton trousers that he still wore girded with twine about the knees, with a waistcoat worn even in a heatwave, a panama hat bought at some ancient rummage sale of Mr. Lucas's, and the countrified brain that is cunning crude, but little more.

They drove into Surrey.

Now the wild roses went everywhere and the white lace of cow's parsley was thrown across the ditches like some shimmering counterpane. The rhododendrons were at their best, cerise and soft mauve, exciting Griselda's interest. One came round unexpected corners on to

127

glades of them. Then at last there was the approach to Wetherley itself, the silver birches blowing in the light wind, and about the district that gracious manner which was indeed part of the house.

As they turned in at the big gate of Wetherley with its small squat lodge on one side, and beyond the drive leading up to the house, Charles purred approval.

'This is Pomp and Circumstance,' he said. 'Oh, I am so glad that you married money, Julie; something our family has never done before, and my goodness how we've needed it!'

The even lines of grassland spread into the distance, then through the dappled trunks of silver birches there came the milky gleam of the pool. The white lilies were budding on its surface rising from beds of green leaves, and showing pearl. Seeing it, Charles almost screamed with delight.

'I must do a picture with this background; it is something that I have always dreamt about.'

The car slowed down and approached now at a snail's pace so that the house itself came into sight, with its even windows and the fanlight over the door. In this hour it looked its loveliest.

'Julia, it's wonderful.'

Even Daniel was delighted at his pleasure. 'So glad you like it; we all adore it. It IS a lovely house.'

He stopped before the steps and they got out.

As they did so, horror struck Julia. Charles would notice the picture of Theresa and would ask about her. There was no time to warn him, and he was not the sort of man to take a hint. She should have said something earlier; now it was too late. What could she do? Acting on impulse she decided that the only way out of this was to pretend that she thought she had told him that Daniel had been married before. To treat it as something which did not matter.

Charles took her hand as they went indoors into the hall and across the library where Mrs. Marriner had the drinks waiting for them, Griselda and Daniel were close at hand.

'Show me the lot,' Charles said, 'the place fascinates me.'

The girls went up to Julia's bedroom to tidy and the men in the library got talking. Charles loved the view across to the Hog's Back; he liked the terrace, which in the summer sunshine looked inviting. Daniel, spurred on by the open admiration, did not wait for the girls' return but took his father-in-law round. They went to the big dining-room, which Daniel had always disliked and seldom had used. Instantly Charles was attracted by the warm claret of the carpet, and the pale grey curtains which seemed to melt into the pale grey walls. Then he took in a deep breath of appreciation.

'I like it all,' he said.

'The house has lovely proportions, and even

129

though we don't use this room much (the day of the big dining-room has rather gone by the board) it is a beautiful room.'

Charles wheeled round and looked at the pink marble mantelpiece with the portrait hanging over it.

'Heavens! Look at that!'

'It's a good picture.'

'A good picture? I'll say. It's a wonderful picture. The girl's got the most glorious eyes, a blue which gives the effect of violet. Most unusual. I have seen that combination only once before in my life. Who was she?'

'She was Theresa.'

'And who was Theresa?'

Daniel did not know why he was beginning to avoid the issue. He could as easily have said. 'She was my first wife,' yet he did not say it. 'She was one of us,' he told Charles.

If he admitted that he had married Theresa, he knew that Charles would demand explanations, and want to know more about it. He could not bear questioning. He simply could not take it. The gaucheness and the silence closed in on him, for he was tied to the past. He had committed himself to secrets which were Theresa's, not his. He could not disclose them.

'She's damned pretty.' And Charles went over to the pink marble mantelpiece, and stood there staring up at the eager hunting face. 'She's damned pretty. By God, she WAS damned

130

pretty. Where is she now?

'Dead,' said Daniel, quite brusquely.

'Dead?'

'She died in a train accident in the States.' He tried to say it casually, and only hoped that he was not overdoing it, for he was inclined to use too much emphasis. The damnable part was that he knew he ought to be thankful that Theresa had died in that accident; at the same time he hoped that she had not suffered. Once he had loved her so deeply. Once he had been inspired by her beauty and had hurled himself into a passionate attachment which he had got to forget. How she had tortured him! How she had changed! He had seen those lovely eyes grow shrewd and lose the radiance that had fascinated him. There was so much he had got to forget, but for all that it lingered. She had said: 'You'll never tell, will you, Dan? You must promise me that.' She had been wretchedly ill at the time just out of the nursing home where she had such dismal experiences undergoing a fearful and tormenting treatment. How thin she had been! Hardly beautiful any more; that had been the tragedy. He had said: 'That is a promise. I'll never tell, Theresa.'

He wasn't telling now.

Because of her portrait he had ordered lunch in the little dining-room, even if it was what Mrs. Marriner called poky. He had been aware of the fact that Julia was relieved that they

131

would eat in the small room, for she also had found the portrait alarming and had dreaded questions. Being an artist, Charles would be sure to pounce on the beauty of the picture, for it WAS something. It was, Daniel supposed, absurd that he did not have it taken down, but somehow he couldn't do that. She had been so young, so vivid, so utterly charming when it was painted, and those violet eyes always followed him about the room. All the same he was glad that she had gone. Glad, and ashamed of being glad. But he did hope she hadn't suffered.

★   ★   ★

They met in the small dining-room, where Mrs. Marriner laid a beautiful lunch with a silver bowl of white water lilies in the centre. There was iced soup, veal cutlets in cream, new potatoes, and peas. Asparagus. Neapolitan ice-cream. And the champagne was excellent.

'Now this is pleasant living,' said Charles, 'the sort of life I like, no rows, no bothers, something of everything. Daniel, if I had known your sister was a widow, I should never have married Griselda!'

'My sister has a mere seven hundred a year, or less; she lives at my expense, and even if I am her brother I have to confess that I am convinced she is hardly your idea of the *grande passion*.'

'Oh well! A chap must expect to put up with some disadvantages for what my piece of cold toast in the shape of a bank manager calls "financial security",' said Charles. 'A man can't have everything. Never mind, I've got a poppet for a wife,' and he lifted his glass to Griselda.

She had recovered from the trials and tribulations of their frustrating journey by now, and she looked happy again and quite refreshed.

'You see, that's what youth can do,' said Charles. 'I'm all wobbles about the knees, and bags under the eyes, but not little Griselda! I shall never forget the sheer agony of that journey; then those Customs officers barged their way in, and do you know what one of them . . . ?' He stopped dead. The memory rankled but there were some stories that even Charles could not tell.

'Afterwards,' said Daniel, 'I was going to suggest that you and the bride relax on the terrace while Julie and I go down to take some magazines to Clare. We do this about twice a week.'

'We ought to come and see her with you. I don't want her to think we are being rude.'

'She won't think that. Do what you will for the place is yours and no one will disturb you.'

'Fine!' said Charles, obviously not wishing to move.

Julie and Daniel wandered across to the Dower House with the magazines. They felt superior in the seniority of their marriage, to that of Charles and Griselda. They felt happy that now they had launched out on a period when they were closer, and settling down to marriage. It seemed already a long time since their wedding day. A letter lying on the mat, Julia thought, and the church clock striking twelve, the hour when Cinderella lost her slipper! and she tried to thrust the memory from her. It was idiotic to recall it.

Clare was insistent about the new pigsties. She needed some means of adding to her income, and everyone told her that there was money in pigs. Daniel had already seen too many of her failures and he did not want to help her. He had had plans for the sties and they would cost a considerable sum of money, too much if she intended to discard them immediately. They had an argument, Julia walking out of earshot, for it worried her.

They walked back again across the park and Daniel was in one of his most charming moods. He admitted that he found Charles amusing and at times almost enchanting. One could not help laughing at his absurd youthfulness. To her Charles always had been the dearest person in all the world, now she had wanted Daniel to love him as she did.

They went into the library, the long windows wide open, the breeze coming in and gently moving the curtains like ripples in some backwater far from the main stream. The other two were on the terrace, happy with each other.

'Tea or no tea, I don't think we ought to disturb them,' Julia said.

'Of course not. Being in love is a wonderful experience and I ought to know!'

'You do love me, Daniel?'

'You must never doubt that.' He turned her round so that they were face to face. 'I could not have lived another moment without you, my dearest. If you died, I'd die too because there would be no point in living a single minute longer. That's the way I feel about you.'

They stood looking into each other's eyes, aware that this was a moment which asked no words; then there came the sound of the telephone shrilling. Julia went to take the call. Hoggie spoke from the other end. Hoggie always mistrusted the telephone which she thought was the invention of the devil, but she felt that she had to get in touch because a cable had arrived for Charles which she felt was bound to be bad news. Life with 'Him' had taught Hoggie to expect the worst at all times and in all places. Julia did not share Hoggie's premonitions of disaster, because quite often a cable meant a commission.

'You open it,' she said, 'and read it aloud to me, then we shall know the worst.'

There was some delay, with the obvious sound of an envelope being opened and the clicking of those disturbing National Health teeth of Hoggie's, then her voice again.

'Are you still there, Miss Julie?'

'Yes, what does it say?'

'I knew it was bad news. It says *Baroness has had a stroke. Come immediately. Karl.*'

'WHAT?'

'I told you it was bad news, Miss Julie.'

The girl was bewildered. Surely this could not be true? Although she had told Daniel that one of these days the vigorous old lady would work herself up into such a temper that she'd have a stroke and die in it, it seemed crazy for it to happen now, just when her father and Griselda had got back. When she could speak she said, 'All right, Hoggie. I'll go and tell him. I suppose this means they'll have to go back at once.'

'Oh, but they can't, Miss Julie! I've cooked a chicken, and there's that queen's pudding . . .'

Julia rang off before there was further argument, and she went across the room to Daniel, her legs shaky, aware of a strangely tremulous feeling inside her. It was not that she had liked the Baroness, she had been considerably frightened by her on the occasions when they had met, it was that death was such a dreadfully final affair, and she had herself said that the Baroness would have a stroke and die.

'It's Hoggie. She's had a cable from Karl, I told her to read it to me.'

'Who's Karl?' He had forgotten.

'You remember that major-domo who looked like Mr. Pickwick and ran the Baroness's *Schloss* for her? He has cabled to Charles, because she has had a stroke, and Karl wants them to go back immediately.'

'But how can they? They've only just got here.'

'I think they'll have to go.'

'What a shocking thing! but Griselda being the only child I don't see how they can get out of it.'

'I wonder if he will go,' said Julia speaking her thoughts out loud.

Together they went across on to the terrace. As they came out of the house into the open air they could see the Hog's Back fading in that beautiful dragon-fly haze of summer time. The newly-weds had dozed off on the canopied hammock, arms about each other. Charles was breathing heavily, his stomach rising rather like some miniature Wrekin, Griselda curled up against him, one long flaxen pigtail unpinned and lying across his chest.

Julia said, 'Charles? Charles? There's a message come from Hoggie. She telephoned me.'

He stirred, opened his eyes and pushed the coarse red hair off his brow. Then he looked at his wrist-watch.

'Heavens! It's late. I must have dozed off. A message from Hoggie, did you say? What on earth could she want?'

'Come over here and I'll tell you.' He looked mystified but obediently came and she took him to the far side of the terrace, for she did not want to break the bad news too suddenly for Griselda. She slipped her hand into her father's arm. 'A cable has come from Karl and I made Hoggie read it out to me. The Baroness has had a stroke and Karl wants you to go back immediately.'

'Good God!' In agony he stared at her, for a moment dumbfounded. 'I won't take that filthy journey again. Heavens! What a journey it was! The Baroness can get on with her stroke, and if she dies, she dies, that'll be just too bad for her. She's had a pretty good run for her money, if you ask me. No, I WON'T go. I couldn't bear it.'

'But there is Griselda to be considered, Charles.'

'Oh Lord! I'd forgotten that, too newly married, I suppose. I bet that old woman did this on purpose; it is just the sort of thing she would do!'

'We've got to tell Griselda.'

'It'll upset her.'

'It would upset anybody but all the same she must be told. I'll help you, Charles,' and they went back together. Griselda was sitting in the hammock trying to pin up the flaxen plait. Daniel, much disturbed, was trying to talk naturally to her and being as unnatural as possible. Julia sat down by her side.

'Griselda, Karl has sent a cable to Charles. Hoggie rang me up and she read it to me.'

'You mean something is the matter with *Müttchen?*' and she stared round-eyed in horror. 'She's dead?'

'Oh no, Griselda, she isn't dead, but she has had a stroke and Karl wants you to go back immediately.'

'Yes, yes. Of course.' She rose almost mechanically, and stood there her fingers twisted together, and quivering.

'Now, look here . . .' Charles began, then saw the look in Julia's eyes, in Daniel's too, and recognizing their disapproval he turned from them muttering to himself, 'As though the one foul journey wasn't enough! Then this has to happen! God's in His Heaven and all's wrong with the blasted world, if you ask me!'

It was Daniel who finally talked him round. He took over with authority and made the arrangements with the calm unflustered ability of a man who understood the situation and knew what was needed. Griselda wanted to fly out to Innsbrück at once, otherwise she did not suppose that she would ever see her poor dear *Müttchen* alive again. Charles thought it wasn't that much urgent, but Daniel did not listen to him, being on Griselda's side, and they made their plans. Daniel telephoned the airport for her; he had a special friend there, someone who once before had helped him, getting him tickets when he thought it was impossible. He went to the telephone and got in touch with Archie Duke. All the time Charles stood muttering and scowling. He could not believe that any of this was true.

He said, 'My first flight will be my last. They say it's a quick way of dying, but I bet you live an eternity in one split second, and I don't want any of my seconds crammed as damned full as that! I won't go. I just won't go.'

Ultimately with everything arranged and nobody listening to him, they went back in the Jaguar to the house to pick up the luggage, for Daniel's friend had worked the oracle. Archie Duke would have tickets ready for them on the evening plane out. Julia helped Griselda pack what she needed, because Hoggie would be no help to anyone in this. Her supper was spoilt. She was furious, She was back at 'Be Thou my Guardian and my Guide', and the defiant smell of burnt chicken lingered about the house.

When the girls came downstairs again with everything settled, Daniel had used all his charms to persuade Charles into his pre-view dark blue suit ready to fly away. His face was that of one stunned.

'This damned suit has been to so many pre-views that my post-view is definitely shiny,' he said, but seeing that the news was obviously grave he had taken the precaution to slip a black tie into the pocket, and with it the crêpe arm band that he had worn when King George the Sixth had died. They would go down well in Austria where they went in for funerals in style, he understood.

They ate a little of the chicken which was not burnt; there was just sufficient time and it would appease the irritated Hoggie, they hoped, then Charles actually kissed her good-bye. He said it was the last time she would ever see him; she could help herself to any picture in his studio that she fancied, and a nice bit of silver to go with it, the moment the news of the plane crashing came over the wireless.

'And think of me kindly, bless your heart, ducky!' said he as he walked gallantly out to the Jaguar, like a man going to his execution.

They drove to the airport.

'We were lucky to get those two seats,' Daniel said, 'would never have done it if I hadn't known old Archie Duke. He is something high-up in the scale at the airport. I've never forgotten when he got me my own urgent flight to the States once.'

'You'll regret getting me into the air when you have to pay for my funeral, because I'll come down again, and fast!' said Charles with profound gloom.

Griselda had gone silent. She was actually worried to death for *Müttchen*; it hurt her that perhaps the row they had had, had brought on the stroke, and the poor lamb would die. She

141

did not know why she thought of Müttchen as a 'poor lamb' (it was the last thing she was), but that was how she felt at the moment. They should not have married so quickly; they should have waited.

They parted at the barrier, nobody sorry that the time had come, for now Daniel and Julia were getting tired of it. Charles and Griselda went out to the plane, whilst Julia and Daniel climbed up to the balcony whence they could watch the departure.

'I do hope it isn't too awful for Charles.'

'He'll like it when he gets airborne. It's people like Charles who make all that fuss, then can't get over the fact that it feels jolly nice after all.'

'It was good of you getting those tickets for them. I do thank you.'

'Archie's always a help.'

She stood staring at the plane which taxied along the ground, then rose, gained height and now prepared to turn into the right direction. 'What was the urgent journey he got you fixed up for, Daniel?'

'One of those things,' his voice had automatically gone quiet; he recognized it and then added more. 'It was at the time of the accident.'

'What accident?'

'The train smash, when Theresa was killed.'

'I see.'

142

The plane was becoming smaller, a dot, a smudge, it was going away from them. They turned from the balcony and went down the steps again, to the ground floor where all manner of people were standing in groups. A magazine stall was selling magazines with highly coloured covers, and a chocolate stall was illuminated. Julia knew that once again she had rushed it; she had wanted to know about that train accident, where it had been, if Theresa was killed outright, and what had happened, but she had forced it, and Daniel still would not be forced. As they drove away she believed that he would never tell her. She was beginning to lose heart, and knew it.

What do I do? she asked herself unable to find words out loud. She was recalling the message in that wretched letter, the letter that had refused to die. *Living to regret it.* Could that be true?

CHAPTER EIGHT

It was a lovely week even if complete silence came from Austria; this was a case of no news being good news, they told each other, for it meant that the Baroness still lived. There was a heat wave, yet not an unbearable one, and Julia was not too anxious lest Daniel had a return of his earlier attack from it.

143

They spent a lot of time working on the site of the new rock garden, something which interested them both, and they enjoyed the cool of the evening when together, almost automatically they went out there.

Daniel was the perfect lover.

The first weeks of their marriage had been difficult when they had kept trying to go back into the past, but now, with no actual promise, they seemed to have decided to put that behind them, and to avoid mentioning it. This meant fewer moods; it meant happier hours. Clare was away on a holiday with a friend which meant that they were far more alone together and could enjoy each other. Julia lived for the moments when he turned to her; in that mood there was no barrier. She could almost forget that Theresa had ever existed. She was falling in love with Wetherley, beginning to enjoy herself in rearranging some of the rooms, but she always felt that Mrs. Marriner hated her interference though the woman said nothing. On the other hand the daily women were amiable and talkative, particularly Cathie Hawkes who would do anything for her.

'I n'ver mind extra work,' Cathie said. 'I wants to help. J'arsk me any t'me.'

Julia could not see herself asking Cathie for extra work, or to stay late. She was a charming idiot, entirely willing, but fatuous, and boring. Her conversation was difficult to follow owing to some articulatory defect which made it difficult for her to speak plainly. 'I'll ask you when I want you, I promise,' she said.

★ ★ ★

One night when they had done a hard day's gardening on the new rock garden, and had had dinner and were sitting on the terrace, Daniel turned to her without a word and kissed her, clasping her almost as if he would hurt her. When she recovered a little, her hand smoothing his hair, she opened her eyes and looking across his shoulders knew that Mrs. Marriner was standing framed in the french windows. She stood like a statue. Her usually impassive face had a look of sheer horror on it, and she was making no attempt to conceal her feelings. Generally she had the inscrutable expression of a cold woman, but now on the instant she betrayed a warm depth, something profound, something passionately distraught which was a challenge. Aware that she had been seen, she turned and walked away making no sound, though the quietness in itself was disturbing. Mrs. Marriner had the air of a wraith but there had been the hatred of the devil in her eyes, and the bitterness of that anger alarmed Julia.

In an awed voice she said, 'Daniel, Mrs. Marriner was standing there and watching us.'

'Nonsense, how could she have been? I expect

she came in with some message or other, saw what was happening, and then did not want to bother us.'

But still Julia hesitated. 'I suppose she was never in love with you? That sort of thing can happen.'

'In love with me? Why should she have been?' His brow knitted for a moment almost as though he was angry with Julia for asking so foolish a question. 'No, of course she was never in love with me.'

'She looked odd. Different. Rather frightening.'

'She's all right. She has had a dreadful life, poor soul, and that has probably brought pain and bitterness into her life. People cannot endure intense suffering without feeling it in the long run.'

'But how did you know that she endured it?'

'Really darling, aren't you being a tiny bit odd about all this? Clare told me. She works with a lot of societies and things and that was how she came into contact with Mrs. Marriner. She told me of her and arranged for her to come here. I suppose she is odd in some ways, certainly she prefers to work alone and got rid of all other resident servants. Quietly, you know. She never makes a fuss, though she doesn't mind the dailies.'

'Did she live here alone with you? Just the two of you?'

'What things you think of, darling! No, of course not, Clare was here.'

There was a silence, an uncomfortable one, then in an effort to break the barrier down, Julia said what she thought. 'I just got the feeling that she was in love with you, hated you kissing me, and wanted you for herself.'

'If she did, then she put her money on the wrong horse. She can't be far off fifty, I imagine.'

'Yes, I suppose so.' She found herself making excuses for Mrs. Marriner, and did not know why she should do this. 'That seems awfully old to us now, but I wonder if we shall think it so old when we are nearly fifty. People do grow unaware of their age, don't they?'

'Yes, they do. But look here, I don't want you to run off with a lot of silly ideas about Mrs. Marriner, because they aren't true. She's been a great help to me, and is a good friend, and what's more I don't want her to find that you don't like her.'

'I'm not jealous if that's what you mean.'

'Good girl,' and he kissed her.

His kisses were impulsive, something he could not hold back, and with the months he seemed to have grown even warmer towards her and to have come closer. She told herself to dismiss the subject; she might have caught Mrs. Marriner at a disadvantage, one of those moments when she had not meant to be watching, but had come as Daniel said with a message, and just hadn't turned away. One did imagine things so often. The great secret of living life satisfactorily was to live for now and let outside anxieties take care of themselves.

Yesterday was dead, the tomorrows were all that mattered, and she must ask no questions about Mrs. Marriner or about Theresa if it came to that.

In the next few hours Mrs. Marriner gave no sign that she had stood there watching the two of them in each other's arms, or that she had realized that Julia was aware of her presence. She did not for a moment betray anything that she was thinking, something she had probably learnt when she had lived in occupied Holland. It meant that one never really knew what sort of a woman she was, but she worked well for them, and her private life was her own.

Yet Julia had been startled by the malignancy of her look. A husband had been caught kissing his wife and Mrs. Marriner had been horrified in some extraordinary way of her own. It was quite inexplicable.

If only things were easier to forget! she thought.

★   ★   ★

Clare was still staying in Worcester and every day in her absence Daniel and Julia went across

148

to the Dower House to see that the woman was airing it properly, that the cats were being fed and that no burglars had broken into the place. It was the house with those weird stumps standing around it in a Druids' circle of death.

'They always make me feel a bit eerie,' Julia said.

'I know. An apple tree in blossom is such a lovely thing; in fruit it is friendly, but its broken old stump is quite awful,' Daniel told her. 'I'll get one of our men to root them up and take them away.'

'You shouldn't do that. I wouldn't want her to think I had been the cause of anything like that.'

'She won't think that. She knows that I hate them too, and after all the Dower House *is* mine. I can do what I like with it. I cannot think why she didn't let the trees be, perhaps it was because she knew I loved them, was vexed with me about something and turned on me that way. Clare can be odd at times.'

They walked back across the parkland. Already the evenings were beginning to shorten; the grass at country roadsides was growing grey and hoary, straggling crazily. The leaves that had once been light green with spring had darkened when the summer passed its meridian. This, Julia thought, is the loveliest summer of all my life; yet it has been an uneasy summer, too.

149

They say the first year is the worst, she thought, but a trifle sadly.

News came from Austria. Charles had adored the flight, and had now decided never to travel any other way. When they got to the *Schloss* the Baroness was better; she had used such revolting language that they had been sent for; she said that strong wine was the cure, insisting that Karl should bring it to her in buckets.

At this rate she is bound to have another stroke, Charles wrote, *but is recovering from the present one. We shall stay about a fortnight, I imagine, then return. She is stuck in bed and we have the Schloss to ourselves which is pleasant.*

The fortnight went on into a month.

Julia and Daniel were spending the time busying themselves with the new garden, contented and happy. She had never realized the joy of an association when two people were so content. Theresa seemed to have gone farther and farther away. She did not matter so much as once she had done, and becoming more settled Julia was able to dismiss the memory of the letter which she had received the night before her wedding. She would not let her marriage lines distress her further, and those earlier days when Daniel seemed to withdraw from her making her aware of a barrier between them, were gradually fading out. He had passing moods but they were not of the man himself but of a silence that he felt bound to keep. He had told her so. In deference to that silence she no longer wondered, 'Did Theresa do this?' or 'do that?' or 'come here and go there?'

Perhaps for a while she had magnified anxieties, and had enlarged her own emotions so that they had tormented her. Now she was wiser. The new feeling of maturity held her; she and Daniel grew fonder with every hour and the result was that many of those first doubts were dying away.

But it did worry her that Daniel was at times much concerned about some of the companies with which he had connections, the Swedish one in particular. He was constantly delayed in London at board meetings, and now feared that the time would come when he had to visit Stockholm which he was making a wild attempt to avoid.

'But I could come, too?' Julia suggested.

'I don't think you'd like it. At this time of the year Stockholm is astonishingly dull, and I would be at meetings all day leaving you stuck in one of their hotels which you'd find quite boring and very lonesome.'

Yet on that very day the office in London had phoned for him, and when he returned from talking to them she knew that he was anxious.

'Something gone wrong?' she asked.

'Stockholm again.'

'It doesn't mean you'll have to go out there?'

'Could be.'

'Oh, Daniel, I do hope not.'

'So do I, and I'll do my damnedest. That's what I'm going up to town about right now.'

She decided to spend the day in the garden. The new rock garden was getting on so well and if she could dig over the top bed, the place where they intended the proposed stream to begin, that would surprise Daniel when he came back. They wanted to dig out a deep pool, and from this the water would flow through the garden which itself was on an incline, dropping in little waterfalls to the lower pool at the far end. It would be very picturesque.

The afternoon was cooler than it had been recently and ideal for the work. She had changed into cotton shorts and a sleeveless blouse, and she went up to the rock garden to work very soon after lunch was done. It had rained sufficiently during the night to make the sandy soil dig more easily, and she must have been in the right mood for she went down quite deep.

She was amazed at her own headway, pleased, for she knew that it would surprise Daniel when he returned, and if he was having a tricky afternoon this might give him some sense of contentment.

Suddenly the earth itself seemed to change.

She heard the noise of something chattering

152

against her spade with a sharply discordant note. She dug more and it did it again. She reached down into the hole and feeling with her hands brought up a broken bottle, staring at it for half a moment, then flinging it aside into the rhododendrons. Then she went on with the work again, going down and down. The sound came back. It was the rattle of glass splintering against her spade, and feeling for it she reached up another bottle of the same dimple pattern, one that she recognized as having once contained whisky. Daniel did not like spirits and always said so; he had never touched them when she was with him, although in France he had taken an occasional cognac after dinner; otherwise he always drank wines.

'I lived too long on the Continent when a boy' he once told her when she mentioned it (Charles generally drank spirits), 'everyone always drinks wine over there. You get used to it. In Rome you do as Rome does.'

She continued digging, yet one after another the bottles came up, some hopelessly broken, some complete, all empty. She left off counting when she reached fifty, for now a certain uneasiness had come to her. It was frightening. Perhaps she was tired and had dug too long, and she sat down for a short rest.

The bottles must have been left behind by a previous owner, she supposed, and it was ridiculous to let them disturb her. But they did disturb her. Daniel's father, and then his brother, had been the previous owners.

As she rested, tired and disheartened, she got the feeling that someone was watching her, that instinct that comes to all, the legacy from some existence before evolution won man from the animals. It told her that she was not alone.

She looked round sharply, ashamed to realize that she was afraid, and she saw Mrs. Marriner standing there. Obviously she had come to tell Julia that tea was waiting, and seeing she was recognized came closer. She looked at the pile of bottles which had been dug up, and then away again.

'Tea is on the terrace, madam.'

'I'll come. Look what I've found!'

'Yes, madam,' but without surprise.

'Someone must have buried them here, all together like that,' said Julia and then she saw the expression on Mrs. Marriner's face, one of those inexplicable looks which made her something of a sphinx, only this time it was quite easy to know what she was thinking. Someone had drunk these bottles dry. Someone Julia knew. It was written there on her face, yet she did not say it; she stood a moment, those hands of hers folded on her stomach, then she turned away.

'So now you know, madam,' was what she said.

So now she knew, *what?*

154

There was inference in this tone even though she said it quite naturally; there was a certain malignance in her eyes, the look of a hunted animal, of a trapped animal, of something that knew despair and hatred and venom all at once. Had she learnt all that in Holland at the time of the occupation?

Mrs. Marriner, like a woman in one of the cheap dramatic films, turned away and walked back to the house without hurrying.

One thing was quite definite. Mrs. Marriner could not have buried the bottles, and most certainly they did not belong to her. Julia's mind went on ahead, she did not want it to go ahead, but it went before she could stop it. Could it be that the empty whisky bottles explained Daniel's moods? The moments when she failed completely to understand him? When he seemed to have travelled so far from her that he was out of reach of her hand, behind some barrier that she could not tear down, nor could she gather what it was? He certainly did not drink whisky, she thought he did not like it, but the bottles she had dug up were hard facts. Somebody must have drunk them empty.

She hesitated, ashamed that such an idea had ever suggested itself to her, and even more appalled that it might be true. She had to recognize that possibility. *So now you know, madam... You know nothing about him and you'll only live to regret it.* She placed the two

155

phrases side by side and hated herself for doing it. She stared after the woman who walked back to the house in that sickeningly unhurried way of hers with her lovely hands folded before her. At this moment Julia's personal feeling were anything but calm, and the casual indifference of the woman seemed to be almost an insult.

Why had she ever thought of digging out that bed? It would have been so much better if she had never found the wretched bottles, and she began to rake over the earth again in a pitiful attempt to cover them. She was tired and did not progress well. She raked the soil over them towards her, because then she could pretend that she had never uncovered them.

If Clare had been here and had been more approachable, perhaps Julia could have turned to her about this, but instantly she abandoned the idea of any help from that channel. She must keep the secret, and she hated herself for believing that it had any association with Daniel, with his sudden incomprehensible changes, with the barrier, with himself.

Half an hour later she left the badly dug patch, the earth raked over and covering it, and she went to the terrace for her belated tea. It must have been replaced for it was still hot. Nobody could ever say that Mrs. Marriner was not good at her work, but somehow now Julia did not want the tea. She knew that Mrs. Marriner would notice that she had eaten nothing, and perhaps that would please her, which was irritating, but what could she do? Restlessness obsessed her. It was difficult to stay still, a foot jumped, her fingers twitched, the uneasiness would not let her be, and she felt for a moment she had stood on the threshold of a horrifying discovery, yet prayed she had dreamt it and none of it was really true.

Yet when Daniel returned he was in such a charming good humour that she almost forgot this, sweeping it away as though it was a passing nightmare to be abandoned in the light of a sunny morning. They went out in the car together with a picnic supper tucked into the back, going out into the wild lands to eat it on the edge of a little copse where the willow herb, once so rosy, was flitting away in tiny tassels of silver swansdown.

'How fast the year is going!' Julia said. 'It always seems that the minute the daffodils come, the dahlias are not far behind.'

'What does it matter? We shall grow old together. Winter and summer are nothing at all.'

'Will you love me when I have wrinkles?'

'For ever, my heart!'

They lingered late till a crescent moon rose above the copse and the world was silvered by starlight. They drove home talking of his childhood, the games he used to play and how then he had envied the brother who would one day inherit Wetherley. In the end it had come to him. Of her childhood, and the almost provocative hazy financial arrangements; the supreme joy of a portrait sold, and that meant they were in the money; the agony when the bank manager had to be approached yet again. The old bank manager had been a pet, easily persuaded by Charles, and not at all like the new man, thin as a rake and white as a nicotiana, and always looking down his nose in the discussion of overdrafts. ('Though the ruddy bank lives on the things,' Charles had said, 'so what the hell DO they want?')

Daniel drove the car into the garage, then they walked across the dewy grass to the house, his arm in hers.

'With all our lives before us, darling,' he said, 'a long march through it, but together. Remember Yeats's lines? *But one man loved the pilgrim soul in you.* I suppose I felt about you that way from the first. You were a pilgrim at Stratford, maybe I was a pilgrim, too, that was the way I shall always feel.'

'What did Yeats say?' she asked.

He quoted it calmly,

'How many loved your moments of glad grace,
And loved your beauty with love false or true;
But one man loved the pilgrim soul in you,
And loved the sorrows of your changing face.'

158

'Daniel, my darling,' was all she could say, for these were emotions so tense that she could not put them into words.

She could forget about the buried bottles now! She could forget that haunting letter and Mrs. Marriner's face, and the red-headed girl with a black velvet riding cap in her hand, lovely Theresa when she had first come to Wetherley. She could forget everything, only remember *One man loved the pilgrim soul in you*, and that was what mattered.

They went indoors together.

★   ★   ★

Julia never expected that Daniel would have to go to Sweden so suddenly. The meeting in London that afternoon had been gruelling. He had tried to postpone it, but had failed.

'It will be for at least a fortnight, could be longer,' he told her late that night on his return.

'But Daniel, it is so sudden. When do you go?'

He hedged. 'It was just that things came to a head sooner than I had thought possible. It is vital if the situation is to be changed, that I go immediately.'

'You mean this week?'

'I mean tomorrow.'

She said, 'Oh no,' with a little gasp, and knew that she had gone quite white.

'Don't think I want to go, darling, I feel it is the end, but it just must be.'

'I couldn't come with you?'

'I tell you, you'll hate it if you do. Your father and Griselda ought to be back fairly soon; the old woman cried wolf about her stroke I am sure, or Karl lost his head and cabled for them when he shouldn't have done. It can't be many days.'

'I suppose not,' and yet for some idiotic reason she was numb with fear.

'Darling, it is just the parting that is so awful. Nothing more. Let's be very brave about this, not even say good-bye.'

She clung to him, crying a little. 'I could never say good-bye to you, Daniel.'

'Nor I to you. I'll be back the moment I can, I promise that. Just wish me luck and quick return. That is what matters most.'

She kissed him again and again. It was so absurd to think that she could not possibly bear it but that was the way it was.

'Good luck and quick return,' she whispered.

Yet when Charles and Griselda returned to the house in the Weald she had been alone at Wetherley for a whole week. The fact that Clare was still absent seemed to have added to her personal loneliness, something she would never have thought could happen. Clare had been away from home most of the summer because she adored paying visits to old school friends.

160

Her absence explained why the argument between herself and Daniel about the erection of new pigsties at the Dower House had fallen into something like abeyance.

Julia had made up her mind to try to persuade Daniel to give them to his sister. This had been such a happy summer. She was drawing so much nearer to him, and they had buried the ghost of any difficulties at the beginning and the least she could do was to try to help other people to something of happiness themselves. 'I'll get him to do it,' she promised herself.

★　　　★　　　★

Julia felt dismally alone. She longed for Daniel's return, and for Charles and Griselda to fly back to the Kentish home. She had not dared confess to her husband that before he left and for no reason at all save a perhaps crazy premonition, she had quite dreaded the thought of being alone in this big house with Mrs. Marriner. They had never warmed to each other. It had almost seemed that as she grew more attached to Daniel in the completely happy phase of fondness which perhaps succeeds the first ebullience of falling-in-love, the gap between herself and Mrs. Marriner had widened.

She blamed herself. She should never have asked the housekeeper about Theresa. She had started off on the wrong foot and it could easily take months to put it right again. She knew that.

Mrs. Marriner fulfilled her duties to the letter; she was zealous, nobody could say that any woman worked harder, but her personality was granite. She was unapproachable, and completely unyielding. Even Daniel admitted that.

In many ways Wetherley was a strange house; it was warmly amiable in itself, and truly a gracious lady, yet it harboured hard people. There was Clare who never broke the surface of her emotions, allowing no one to pierce down into her depths and share life with her. Daniel, who at moments was the ardent lover and adorable, yet at others could draw away half sulky and almost a stranger to the girl who loved him.

I'm growing-up, she thought, I'm changing too, and in time all this will right itself. I am sure of it.

But she did not think any time would change Mrs. Marriner's reactions to her. Ever polite, always ready to obey a command but never allowing one bit more to be discovered about herself.

The first week when Daniel was away had dragged terribly.

It was beautiful weather with the garden at its best; the michaelmas daisies were in lavender lanes in the borders, and the Aaron's rod hedge-

162

high. The asters were great rivulets of purple and cerise flaunting along the border edges, the big shaggy kind that Daniel loved most, Julia as well. She tried to get ahead with the new rock garden when she could, but the weather was very hot, and they had come to the more difficult part where the work was tiresome. Also she seemed to tire very easily. She ordered from a London library a lot of boooks she wanted to read, and when they arrived they were an engaging package, yet somehow concentration was evasive. Even the television became boring.

One day she drove the car over to the Weald and went to call on Mr. Lucas at the vicarage. He was not the man she would have chosen, for he could be embarrassingly shy, but she had the longing to meet somebody she knew, thought of him, and on the spur of the moment went over to see him. Loneliness drives hard.

Mr. Lucas asked her to share his very indifferent tea, and they talked of local affairs; when she left he did not ask her to return if she felt alone, but he did ask for a contribution to his latest charity which was doing badly.

On the step he said, 'I do envy you your housekeeper. These days it is madly difficult to get anyone to work for you, and for the last week I've had to do most of the chores myself. You're lucky.'

'Mrs. Marriner can be difficult,' parried Julia.

'But can't they all? Can't WE all, if it comes to that? You hang on to her. It's murder getting outside help these days.'

'I'm sure it is,' she said.

She called in at her father's house where Hoggie was having a vigorous turn-out. She looked up with her beady eyes.

'My goodness, Miss Julie, you're looking downright peaky,' was her greeting, 'not at all well I'd say, whatever have you been doing to yourself? Tst, Tst, Tst,' and off went the old false teeth into vigorous action.

'I'm all right, thank you.'

'Well, you don't look all right to me, and that's a fact,' she said. 'Doing far too much. I suppose none of your servants work for you proper? I know what they are these days. And that housekeeper you've got what looks like a jackdaw. Tst, Tst, Tst.'

'They work hard. Mrs. Marriner may look like a jackdaw, but I must say she does her job amazingly well.'

Hoggie had been taken over to Wetherley on a voyage of discoveries, wearing her best coat and the hat with the bunch of cotton violets in it, and obviously completely ill at ease. She had said little at the time, but had inspected Mrs. Marriner of whom she heartily disapproved and on the way back had made a few acid comments. 'Him' would never have had her near him. Not with a barge pole he wouldn't, she had said.

164

'She never spoke to me when I come over,' she announced, 'not that I wasted me time on her, not me! I've met her sort before, and I know what she is.'

'She had an awful time in Holland during the war, when the Nazis were after her,' Julia said.

'If you ask me, nobody's ever been after her, and that's her trouble!' and Hoggie's voice dropped into a sinister whisper. 'Man-mad. Oh, I knows them sort. I don't believe a word about all that business in Holland; nor about them Nazis neither. It takes some of us that way. Though not me of course, I'm respectable, I am. Man-mad is her trouble. It sticks out a mile.'

'Oh, I don't know about that,' said Julia, trying to pass it off and profess loyalty to a woman who at least served her well.

'Well, I do. I'm older than you, and I knows,' said Hoggie in one of her difficult moods, 'and you ought to have one of them Seidlitz powders if you asks me. Plain ill you looks. It worries me to see you that peaky.'

Julia did not stay very long for the conversation seemed to be limited. She did not want to discuss Mrs. Marriner, and it was hardly inspiring being told how ill she looked. Next morning, very possibly as a result of Hoggie's insistence, she woke up first thing feeling desperately sick. This has been willed on me, she told herself.

She knew what it was, of course, because as a child she had suffered from periodical bilious attacks and if she had had any sense she would have acted on Hoggie's advice and taken the Seidlitz powder. She was limp all day, lying on the terrace hammock until she felt better. By tea-time she was very much recovered.

It had to be that very afternoon that the first big trouble began. Only these few days since Daniel had been away and perhaps a fortnight ahead till his return, and this started. After tea Mrs. Marriner brought her in the weekly accounts and laid them on the desk, the books with them. She was pedantic about these; she wrote in a form of printing, always beautifully done and extremely easy to read, crossing the t's and dotting the i's and giving the prices plainly. Daniel had said that so far he had never found a single mistake in her addition which said something seeing she had been here so long.

After dinner Julia saw them lying on the desk and she opened them. The evening had turned cooler with the habit of late summer, and she was glad of the pleasant fire. The time of year had come when it looked welcoming, and she drew her chair up to it. When she had done the coffee she began to go through the books.

Sometimes she wondered why she ever looked at them, for after all they were so sure to be accurate and her own arithmetic was extremely hazy. Here were all the details, distressingly clear, and she did not know why they worried her. At home she had never looked at the books. Charles's idea was, 'Well, if Mr. Bun the baker is going to cheat us, he'll cheat us somehow, so why worry?' and he hadn't worried. She felt that it was quite dreadful to be young, sitting here and wasting time on the things that did not really matter. Mr. Bass who brought the milk, the eggs and the cream; Graham the Frimley butcher; Dawkins who delivered the flour and cakes sometimes when Mrs. Marriner was not baking, and every day the bread.

Each entry had been endorsed in that curiously exact printing of Mrs. Marriner herself.

Julia was half way through when a note fell out of the book, something that apparently Mrs. Marriner had forgotten. The note was a scribble, done in a hurry, and had been intended for the milkman but had been mislaid. Mr. Bass had never received it. Once lost, Mrs. Marriner had given up looking and must have scribbled out another one.

Seeing the note Julia was almost spellbound, for the writing suddenly prompted her memory. It was exactly similar to that letter she had picked up from the cottage doormat the midnight before her wedding. It was identical. Staring at it, she went cold with amazement, with horror and with an abiding resentment.

Then the veil fell from her eyes and for the

first time she saw the truth with a startling clarity. She remembered those moments when Mrs. Marriner had found Daniel's arm about her, and that evening on the terrace when he had been kissing her. She remembered the look in those furtively dark eyes; the frustration which drenched them. This woman had been starved for the very emotion of which Julia had so much; she longed for love. Could it be that Mrs. Marriner who had been here when Theresa had died, comforting him, protecting him, caring for him, had believed that one day he might be her own? She might be older and he considerably younger, but even then it might have been that.

Mrs. Marriner had made everything easy in Daniel's life, she had made him domestically content, and in caring for his creature comfort had hoped perhaps that the hour would come when he gave her a more permanent position at Wetherley. It never came, for Daniel went to the Memorial Theatre to return a ticket that he could not use, and lost his heart.

That was undoubtedly what had happened.

Once when Julia had been visiting Clare, and together they had gone to feed the chickens in the orchard, Clare had said, 'You know, I used to think that Daniel would one day marry Mrs. Marriner. It's funny, but I guess she thought so too.'

The remark had registered nothing at the

168

time, but it did now. The truth was clear, almost burningly so as she turned it over in her mind.

She thought about that wedding of hers, the dining out with Daniel the previous night, the hurry home to get back before midnight, and going into the empty cottage to find the letter. Now when she went into it, it was all clear. Mrs. Marriner often drove over to Aldershot to shop in that tiny car which Daniel had given her; she went all over the place in it and nothing would have been easier than for her to drive over to the Weald in a last frantic effort to stop the marriage which would menace her life so much. Probably she knew that both of them would be dining out, she would have pressed Daniel's suit for the occasion. He could even have told her about it, for men in love like to talk about the girl who interests them.

How Mrs. Marriner must have hated me! Julia thought. All along she had been trying to convince herself that she had imagined the dark looks, now she knew the truth. She herself had been a sword thrust into Mrs. Marriner's own heart, because she had ended a dream. The fact that the dream could never have materialized meant little. A woman in love never realizes that. Perhaps the anonymous letter had worried Julia far more than she had liked to admit, certainly it had continued to worry her and now she knew that the relief had come. She understood all about it at last.

Before she could stop herself she rang the bell.

The moment she had done it she felt sickly apprehensive, almost agonized, yet one side of her nature was challenging. This woman was an enemy, someone whom Julia and only Julia herself could confront, however much it demanded of her. (I AM growing up, she thought again, aware that something of the *gamine* was receding from her, and that a new Julia was succeeding it). She shrank from meeting Mrs. Marriner, yet she could not leave this until Daniel came home. He out of loyalty would possibly minimize it, he would never realize how much it meant to her for it was something that men did not understand in the same way, and it was natural for him to see Mrs. Marriner through different eyes.

The door opened almost silently and there she was, black silk dress and white collar to it as always. Those rapacious eyes looked questioningly at Julia. Was there something that she wanted?

'I think this is yours,' Julia said, and she held out the written message for Mr. Bass. She knew instantly that Mrs. Marriner realized what she meant though she gave no outward show of it, merely advancing into the room and quietly taking the scribbled note from Julia.

'Yes, madam, I put it out for Bass yesterday

and then mislaid it. It slipped my memory that it was amongst the books, I thought I must have put it on to the fire.'

'I recognized the writing,' said Julia very slowly and very surely.

'Yes, madam. I bring you the books each week.'

Julia knew that Mrs. Marriner saw what had happened and was trying to put up a smoke screen in her personal defence; Julia blew it aside.

'I did not recognize it from the books, you print them, and this is quite a different type of writing. Once you wrote me a private letter, didn't you?'

Their eyes met.

'I don't think so, madam.' Not in anger, not in alarm, just the evasive answer of a woman who was playing a part.

'You brought that letter to the cottage the night before I married, and you did not sign it.'

A tic throbbed in the woman's cheek, working like a clock with quite horrible automatism; she swallowed, then spoke without tone. 'I don't know what you mean, madam. I had never seen you until Mr. Strong brought you here to lunch on your wedding day.'

'I know, but you brought me that letter.'

Mrs. Marriner was ashen; she seemed to have become strangely thin. 'Perhaps you would rather I left, madam?'

'Yes, I would.' Deliberately Julia threw down the gauntlet. 'I think you had better go tomorrow.'

'Yes, madam, that will be convenient, thank you.' She walked unhurriedly back to the door, the hands still folded on the stomach, apparently undisturbed. From the door she turned, her face now blazing with anger, her eyes vivid fires, her pale mouth aflame.

'I hate you. I have always hated you just as I have always been faithful to him, and you know it. He would have married me if he had never met you, and I would have made up for everything he went through in that dreadful time. You don't know what happened in this place, and he won't tell you, I don't suppose. But I know, and I shall never forget.'

Julia stared at her amazed; she had underestimated the power and the fire. She pulled herself together, it would never do for both of them to lose control. 'I don't know what you suggest happened here, but I don't believe a word of what you say,' she said, yet was aware that her words cut no ice, and that she sounded almost childishly simple against the other woman's hard and bitter discernment.

When Mrs. Marriner spoke again the moment had passed and her tone was quite cold. 'It is true, madam. There is in Wetherley much that you have no idea about. Good night, madam. Good-bye, madam. I think when you discover the truth you will live to regret this.'

The door shut on her again without a sound.

There was something gruelling in the fact that even when she was angry the woman could be so quiet. No footsteps went across the hall, no far door closed; it was just that a moment before she had been venomous, and now was only a wraith, leaving Julia with the sense of frustration.

She could not do the books tonight after all, for her head ached too much; the strain had been great, and because of it she went upstairs to bed. As she went she was afraid that somewhere in the shadows of the hall those dark eyes would be watching her, but there was never a sound. Fear made her imagine things, she thought.

Going into her room she shut the door and turned the key, gasping for the sudden relief this brought. The bed had been turned down, there was a glass of iced water for the night beside it, and the electric fire had been turned on. That would be Cathie Hawkes, who every evening did this routine job here, then went back to her father's drab little cottage across the park. Somehow Julie was glad it had been Cathie: she did not want Mrs. Marriner in the room.

She went to bed, and three hours later woke with the horrible consciousness of being terribly alone. Of terror. The house that Daniel had called a gracious lady had tonight become ominous; Theresa had been here. What was the truth Mrs. Marriner had hinted about in the past when she had been stung to a bitter fury? What had she meant?

When Daniel came back he must tell her everything, she decided, about Mrs. Marriner who lived and Theresa who had died. Now her door was locked and she was safe; she calmed herself and dropped asleep again. She woke late and startled, aware that nobody had called her.

She sprang up realizing that about the house was a sinister quietness. At first she thought it was sleep that made her feel this way, then when her mind cleared she would find everything more usual. She rose, bathed and dressed, surprised that her breakfast tray had not arrived. When she opened the door and stepped out into the corridor there was no sound. The house smelt fetid. None of the windows had been opened, the place was unaired and exactly as it had been last night when she had come up to bed.

She went down, and in bewilderment opened a window to let in the new day. Then she saw the note lying on a silver salver on the side table, and she opened it.

Dear Madam, she read. *I have left. It is wiser and I shall not be looking to you for a reference. Will you kindly send my luggage which is already packed, to my cousin, Mrs. Winter, at 47 Davis*

174

Terrace, Maida Vale?
  Yours truly, Marion Marriner.

When she could bring herself to do it Julia
went up to Mrs. Marriner's room which she had
never entered before. It was extremely tidy;
there were two large trunks strapped and
addressed. Nothing more. The bed had been
stripped, the soiled linen folded neatly and laid
on a chair, a dust cover over the bed itself. She
felt young, lost, and stupidly afraid.

Half an hour later, just when she was
fidgeting over the stove, boiling an egg, making
toast that had burnt and some coffee, Cathie
Hawkes appeared. Cathie was possibly thirty-
four, she could have been any age, and she was
mentally retarded. She limped so that if she was
to walk she had to run bringing her twisted body
awkwardly after her. She had a vacant smile,
accepting life in good part. When she saw Julia
cooking, she gaped and put a clumsy hand over
her horrified mouth.

'Oh my!' said Cathie.

'Mrs. Marriner has left, and I'm getting
myself some breakfast.'

Cathie nodded gawkishly, then became
confidential. 'I thought she'd go. Aw'kard she
was, v'y aw'kard,' and she tied an apron round
herself. 'I'll do that, ma'am.'

'All right. I'll wait in the library.'

'Okay,' said Cathie, her one touch with

175

modernity and something she said freely whether appropriate or not.

She laughed, for nothing gave her greater pleasure than to believe she was important. When she laughed she displayed enormous pale glazed gums, dribbling a little, but catching the dribble with a brisk finger. She was willing, delighted to work but deplorably inefficient. Soon the widowed Rita Forbes would come along, and perhaps she could be persuaded to come and sleep in till Julia got fixed up with another housekeeper. Or Mrs. Bentley, as her sailor husband was in Malta. It was unthinkable to sleep here alone.

At half-past nine she rang up three London registry offices, to find that nobody wanted country jobs. People would not leave London for the country, moddom, they said. She tried Sevenoaks, Aldershot and Bagshot. They would take down her name, but they held out little hope. People did not like the country much. Would they have a car? All the afternoons off? A telly? Their own sitting-room? What advantages could she offer?

To Julia, who was accustomed to Hoggie, there were so few advantages; she had never thought of them.

'The wages are excellent,' she said to the last woman who seemed to be a trifle more human.

'Dey expects it to be good dese days,' she said, much distressed by a violent cold in the

176

head, 'I don't doe what dey do want, I don't.'

At eleven Julia asked Rita Forbes if she could 'oblige'. Mrs. Forbes was roundly small, a hen sparrow of a woman with pert eyes. She looked startled. Apparently she always went out in the evenings because she was interested in old-time dancing. Her gentleman friend had a Bubble car and downright comfy it was! She couldn't sleep in, not under those circumstances, could she? She coloured rather uncomfortably as she said it.

Julia turned to Mrs. Bentley who was a different sort of girl, more friendly and comfortable. She would have loved to help but she didn't see how she could. Not just now, if Julia knew what she meant, for she was helping dad out. Her younger sister was going to have a baby, and she was seeing after the sister because she was a bit funny at times, if Julia knew what she meant. She had been funny the night she had gone into the wood with the strange gentleman, and a lot funnier when she came out the next morning. Mrs. Bentley could not sleep out because most babies got born at night, didn't they? and she supposed this here would be same as that there. If Julia knew what she meant.

Hopelessly fogged, Julia said that she understood perfectly. She panicked. She did not think she could summon up her courage to sleep alone in this big house. Oh, if only Clare had not

177

been away! If only Charles and Griselda had come back!

The panic increased.

She would have gone for Hoggie if she had ever thought that Hoggie would consent to come, but 'Him' would never have permitted that. 'Him' was decrepit; he was bowed and bent, his cord trousers tied with twine on the knees, his rubicund bland face edged by a monkey fringe of imitation chinchilla, his eyes bloodshot. But Hoggie doted on him. She would not desert him.

'"Him" wants me,' she would have said.

Towards midday Julia arrived at the dreadful conclusion that she would have to ask Cathie Hawkes to sleep in. The girl was dotty; there was that unhappy limp; the way she ran bringing a reluctant hip along with a jerk; that awful habit of laughing and displaying all those gums, the silly answers and the adbridgement of the English language to her own use. At the same time Cathie Hawkes it would have to be. Julia called her into the dining-room.

'Yes, m'm,' she said.

'Mrs. Marriner has gone and I want someone to sleep here in the house whilst the master is away, Cathie. Could you come?'

'Me? W't me?' Cathie was enchanted with the idea; all the gums sparkled and the eyes shone. 'Me sleep in a l'dy's h'se, oh my! D'you mean me, m'm?'

178

'Yes, Cathie. You could have Mrs. Marriner's room if you would make up the bed,' and all the time Julia was on edge lest Cathie refused. Cathie was the last chance. Horrible as it might appear to be, she WAS the last chance.

'Me sl'p in M's. Marriner's room? Me? Oh my!'

'Could you do it, Cathie?'

The giggling began; she flung back her silly head, the bird's nest of hair wobbling. 'Okay, I'd love it, m'm. I'd go h'me for me b'fast?'

'Oh no. I wouldn't want you to do that. You would get mine and yours at the same time. It is only until I can get somebody else, it can't be for long.'

'They're difficult,' said Cathie, delighted to pour cold water on the attempt. 'Oh, the m'ney they w'nts!' That evidently gave her a fresh angle on the arrangement. 'You'd pay me a b't m're for sl'ping here?'

'Of course.'

'I th'ght so.' Back came the giggles. 'And me sav'ng for C'stmas and that.'

'But Christmas is months ahead, Cathie.'

'I know. I want a set like l'dies h've. Lace. Dr'p dry and all.'

'I'll give you some,' said Julia on the spur of the moment, egged on by her desperate need. 'Now you get Mrs. Marriner's room prepared for yourself and come back this evening.'

'I'll get your s'per on a tr'y.'

'That would be kind. Your own as well?'

'Yes, m'm. Okay. I'll w'nt some s'per,' and she went off tittering to herself. Julia sank back in blessed relief.

★   ★   ★

She went on telephoning registry offices who could not supply maids. The few housekeepers there were wanted a modern flat with a car, the telly, and no work to be done. They preferred single men. Julia felt hopeless.

At six o'clock Cathie returned triumphantly, running and giggling as she came. There were the sounds of her banging about in the kitchen, nobody would have called her anything but extremely clumsy, though very willing. At half-past seven the evening meal arrived on a tray rather peculiarly arranged, and on it reposed the boiled egg which was Hoggie's stand-by in emergencies. There was some coarse bread-and-butter, and a sloppy blancmange that had collapsed in its dish. Half an hour later Cathie returned for the tray, inquiring excitedly, 'Was it ev'r so l'vly?' Half-heartedly Julia said that it was. Last thing of all Cathie came in to ask if she would like a nice cup of hot cocoa, because she was having one. Julia refused it.

'And ab't the b'fast?' said Cathie, 'I th'k a boiled egg w'd be n'ce.'

'Very,' said Julia. The fight had gone out of

180

her.

Obviously this could not continue long. Cathie was an optimistic half-wit who thought that everything she did was fine. She was not deterred or embarrassed by her mistakes; she never saw them as mistakes. She overslept in the morning, having no idea of the way to set an alarm clock and not liking to ask in case it was 't'k ag'in her.' Julia waking and feeling ill, far more despondent than she had thought possible, wanted to cry.

But soon Daniel would come home.

She must think of that.

She received a letter from him that morning. There had been a lot of trouble in Stockholm. None of the meetings had gone the way that he wanted, which he believed to be vital to the future; this was a case of staying on to see the crisis through, or admitting defeat and getting out with a very serious loss for the shareholders, he was convinced. They had to be considered. He intended travelling north to see the factories, this had to be done and it would probably delay his return for another ten days. Unless something surprising happened; something that he did not anticipate.

I am really very glad that I did not try to persuade you to come out here, darling, because conditions are not good. I am working day and night, and should die if I thought of you being left alone to mope in a hotel. You are better at home, and all blessings on you. It is good to think that Mrs. Marriner is with you for I can always trust her. She's wonderful. Take it from me that I shall be home the moment I can, meanwhile here is all my love . . .

That was when Julia broke down.

CHAPTER NINE

CHARLES and Griselda were coming home.

The Baroness was loath to let them go, and had offered her usual difficulties when they broke the news to her, but Charles had grown sick of the visit. He wanted to paint again. Mrs. Tanner had sent him a sharpish letter from Sevenoaks to inquire when her portrait would be done, she was sick of waiting, and would remind him that she had paid down something on it already. He had no wish to return and paint that particular model, but his hand was being somewhat forced.

In the end he and Griselda left the *Schloss* in a flaming rage for the Baroness had flown into a fury, had thrown things across the room declaring that if they left her now it would force her to marry the first fortune-hunter who offered his hand.

'She's got some hope,' said Charles as they drove away.

They entered the house in the Weald to the tune of 'Rock of Ages' which was something. In a way Charles was glad to be back, and thankful for what was peace compared to the ferment of the *Schloss* and that dreadful woman. This is my day, he thought. They went upstairs to tidy after a trying journey, and came down again to a good sound English dinner of roast chicken and queen's pudding. There was nothing like English food, Charles thought, and he damned to all that bilious *Wiener Schnitzel* and *Apfelstrudel* which you tasted for hours after and then got the hiccups.

With the coffee which he had to admit did not compare with the sort old Karl served up, Hoggie told them how worried he was about poor Miss Julia. Mrs. Marriner had walked out on her (naturally Hoggie had always known she would!), and now she was all alone in that big house save for a dotty daily, who had been persuaded to come in to sleep. Charles announced that privately he had always thought Mrs. Marriner was a bitch, and was really not surprised. Hoggie was repelled by the word.

'But in that great big house,' she said, 'and poor Miss Julie not so well and all.'

'She isn't ill surely?' It was the first that he had heard of this.

'The bile,' said Hoggie clicking her false teeth

183

together as she cleared the table. It annoyed Charles.

'What do you mean "the bile?" And being alone, too? Daniel's got enough to pay for comfort, damn his eyes! What's he doing about it?'

'Gone away, he has. Somewhere awful abroad,' and there was more active work with the false teeth.

'Why don't they get a first-class married couple to go in and run the place for them, like everybody else does who has got the money to pay for it?'

Firmly Hoggie became impressive. 'Because,' she said, 'things isn't what they was, they aren't! We all knows that one, we does. You can't get people to work for you now, that you can't unless she is some old fool like me, you can't.'

'Well, you were the one who said it!' remarked Charles starting on the coffee again. Talk about bitter! Oh, my goodness!

'The days of being waited on hand and foot's gone,' said Hoggie. 'That Mrs. Marriner wasn't half no good, she wasn't. I knew that. I know a good piece of meat when I sees it, and a bad piece of meat too, I does.'

Charles had been about to comment bitterly on this last statement, when he caught Griselda's eye. It was no good embarking on a row the first night home.

Julia had taken Hoggie over to Wetherley one

184

day and Hoggie had gone out of her way to convey her personal private feelings about Mrs. Marriner to Julia. Today nobody would work. If you got somebody at four shillings an hour you was lucky, you was. Then she did what she liked, the way she liked and in her own sweet time, which was a lot of good, wasn't it?

Charles let her rant on.

'Well, aren't you doing something about it?' he asked at last.

Hoggie smirked. She had moments of genius, and 'Him' often told her so. This very day she had heard of someone seeking a domestic job in the neighbourhood. The woman was a stranger working at Penshurst as a caretaker, and leaving in a few days. Mr. Lucas had told Hoggie, and instantly she had asked what about Miss Julie? As he was going over to Penshurst to see the incumbent he had promised to see if Mrs. Dawes at the big house was still free. Both were anxious to help, and apparently Mr. Lucas had left a message in the right quarter. He had seen the woman, he told Hoggie when he passed this evening, she seemed pleased at the idea and said she would ring up Wetherley. Hoggie had had a message of gratitude from Miss Julie.

There was the glory of self-triumph in Hoggie's eyes. 'She's called Gertie Dawes,' she said.

'Well, that ought to take her one big hell of a way!' said Charles, sick to death of the story.

'Mr. Lucas says she looks a bit funny, but she's been ill. Half her face don't work.'

'You mean she's had a stroke and is paralysed?'

'Oh no, not that. She had a bad car accident, and she's a widow.' Off went Hoggie again, just remembering that the washing-up needed attention.

Charles said, 'It would be far better if Julie came here until she is properly settled with a married couple. We'll go over tomorrow and tell her that. Of course she ought to be able to get maids, we'll get her fixed if old Gertie Dawes fails her.'

It was good to be home again. The leaves might be rimmed with that burnt light brown of beech, or the vivid gold of flaunting chestnut, but Charles knew that he was glad to be back. When Hoggie had returned to 'Him' he and Griselda went out to the studio. The heater had been lit and the whole atmosphere of the place was warm and friendly, so that he could sense its welcome, and if the portrait of Mrs. Tanner set on the easel was a reminder that tomorrow he would have to get busy on it, for the moment Charles dismissed the thought.

'I love you, darling one,' he said, 'and God has been good in giving you to me.'

'I pray *Müttchen* is not lonely tonight without us.'

'I wouldn't worry about that. She'll have met

the fortune-hunter perhaps,' and he laughed.

She turned her little face to his and he caressed it tenderly and kissed her. Life was wonderful. This, he thought, is the grandest love story ever. More wonderful to be my age and yet a Romeo again. Much, much more wonderful . . .

★   ★   ★

It was a considerable comfort to Julia to know that Charles had come back home, for if the worst came to the worst she could always go there to stay. His friendly telephone call had put fresh heart into her; his schoolboy exuberance over it all had given her the feeling that she had abandoned herself to foolish miseries and in life it is always darkest before the dawn.

Cathie was settling in and thought that she was doing a stupendous work. She pattered round at Julia's heels until the sound of that jog trot of hers made Julia want to scream. The peaceful leisure and that enviable tranquillity which had been the very soul of Wetherley had vanished in the night with Mrs. Marriner.

A Norwich agency put her in touch with a young couple up north who seemed promising. In her dilemma she rang them up in Newcastle-on-Tyne in the situation they were about to leave. The mistress of the house warned her they were impossible; she had never had a moment's peace with them in the place, and was praying for the moment when they left. She rang up the agency again. They turned offhand; they had nobody else; they were not likely to have anybody else; things were not what they once had been.

Julia felt it would have been different if she had not felt so young, and so unable to cope with it all. She must get Wetherley running properly before Daniel returned; he would never tolerate Cathie's irregular meals and something different must be organized for him.

Then Charles rang her up to tell her that Hoggie had found somebody; she and Mr. Lucas. Her name was Gertie Dawes, and almost immediately after that Gertie Dawes herself rang up and asked for an interview. At last she was getting somewhere. Gertie Dawes sounded reserved, spoke very well, and obviously wanted to get settled quickly.

After she had arranged to send the car over to fetch her, Julia felt quite sick with relief. What would she do if she hated Gertie Dawes on sight? If she was afraid of her? Privately she knew that she was afraid of most of the maids, not Cathie, of course, only she hoped that she did not show it.

She sat in the library waiting for Mrs. Dawes to come. When she heard the sound of the car, she felt sick again, it was absurd to permit herself to get into such a state of nerves, but it was happening. Cathie let her in. Julia heard her coming across the hall to the library, and the door opened. There she was. She seemed to be considerably older than Julia had expected, and much shabbier. She was small, rather pitifully thin with pits under her high cheek bones, and her eyes sunk back into deep sockets half hidden by dark glasses. Julia could see that she screwed those eyes up almost as if the light hurt her, even behind the glasses. Her hair was cut like a man's, thick and sturdy, dead straight and iron-grey the colour of flannel trousers. It lay in ugly slices and she wore no hat.

The brown stuff coat hung badly, but her hands though very thin, lined and creased, were capable hands and she used them well. Julia always noticed people's hands. Mrs. Marriner's had attracted her, lying like flowers together.

Mrs. Dawes looked at Julia, then on the instant the eyes behind the dark glasses went swiftly round the room, taking in every detail sharply, like a bird in flight.

'Good afternoon. Please come in and sit down,' Julia said and indicated the chair opposite to her.

Mrs. Dawes said nothing. She came to the chair and sat on it, going well into it, not on the edge as most people of her type. In fact she seemed far more interested in the room itself than in the mistress of the house.

'Hoggie, our old housekeeper at my father's

189

home, told me of you. I believe Mr. Lucas came to see you on my behalf, which was kind of him.' Julia had practised this with herself, much distressed lest in the interview she should put the applicant off. 'I need someone to housekeep here. There is only myself and my husband— he's away just now.'

'Yes, I understand that.'

'We have three daily women, but the house is large and I know there is an awful lot to do.'

'It's big,' she admitted, but without any sign of irritation.

Alarmed that the size of Wetherley would put her off coming here, Julia explained how helpful the dailies were, and Cathie never minded doing overtime. 'You have done this sort of work before?' she asked, 'I mean you were just the caretaker at Penshurst, Hoggie said?'

Gertie Dawes had done the job before.

She explained rather haltingly that before she had suffered this bad car accident she had been well off. The accident had been alarming and she had been in hospital for months with bad head injuries. That was why she had to wear dark glasses; her eyes hated the light, and if exposed to it she endured excruciating headaches.

'For a time my face was partially paralysed,' she said, then almost as an afterthought, 'my hair went grey overnight.'

'How dreadful for you!'

190

'It was very dreadful. I did some housekeeping in Scotland but the weather was so bad and I wanted somewhere that was warmer. You see I was in California for a time so I missed the sunshine.'

'In California?'

'Yes, madam. Perhaps you would like to read my references?' She opened a shoddy bag and brought out three recommendations clipped together with a paper fastener, that had grown jagged at the edges.

Julia read them and they were excellent. She realized that this woman was extremely capable, that she was lonely, in some way sad. She wanted a home probably. Alas Julia was dwelling on her own need. She heard the sound of Cathie coming at her jog trot across the hall. There was a crash as she dropped the tea tray, and a despairing scream. Julia looked at Mrs. Dawes.

'When could you come to me?'

'I leave Penshurst tomorrow, madam, I could come then.'

'Would you like it to be a month on trial, to see how we like one another?'

'Very well, madam, a month on trial.'

'You'd like to see the house. I'll show you round.' Julia got up and led the way with the contented feeling that at last something had been settled. She went into the drawing-room and on to the big dining-room. 'We hardly ever dine here, these days,' she said. 'We don't entertain in a big way and my husband feels that the tiny dining-room is far more sociable.'

Mrs. Dawes nodded. She was not looking at Julia but about the room, the views from the windows, the long sideboard with the silver on it, and the picture of the red-headed girl with the challenging eyes which hung over the fireplace. Her throat was working.

'That is a very lovely picture, madam.'

'It was my husband's first wife. She died in a train crash in the States, poor thing! She was lovely, wasn't she? She had such beautiful eyes.'

'Yes,' said Mrs. Dawes. Her hand in its cotton glove went to her face for a second, to the paralysed lip which had a tendency to droop. She dabbed it cautiously.

They went all round the house save for the rooms which were not used now. When they came downstairs Mrs. Dawes said little. Julia did not know what she felt about it, and was afraid to ask her lest it annoyed her. Coming into the hall there was the robust back of Cathie on all fours in her faded overall mopping up after the calamity of the tea-tray. It was not a stimulating sight, but thank goodness from tomorrow the running of the place would be in better hands. She took Mrs Dawes to the car and Henry took her back to Penshurst, then Julia returned to Cathie.

'After all,' said Cathie, 'it didn't sm'sh th't

192

much. The br'-an-butter plate, two lit'le ones, and a cup and sa'cer, it isn't much. Oh, AND the m'lk jug. You'd h've exp'ted more, wouldn't you, m'm?'

Julia ignored that. She said, 'Mrs. Dawes is coming to take over Mrs. Marriner's job in the morning. You won't want to go on sleeping here, Cathie, so get her room ready for her, and put some flowers in it. I want to make it nice so that she'll want to stay.'

Cathie sat back on her haunches and stared at Julia. 'Me go'ng? You don't wan' me? an' me so happy?' and she began to cry.

The sight of Cathie laughing was disconcerting, but the sight of her crying was far worse for much more gum was exposed. Julia knelt down beside her trying to console her. She could come every day as she had always done, so why worry? She had been a dear, such a lot of help, and her cooking was just fine. Cathie must not get herself worried about this. Cathie admitted she had thought it was for ever and that was okay! Now nothing was okay and she wept violently.

It was, Julia realized, just about time that somebody else took over. Even if Mrs. Dawes was a little odd, probably the result of that dreadful car accident, you couldn't have everything.

She returned to a somewhat frustrated tea.

It was a boiled egg breakfast next day.

Julia rang up Charles to tell him that she would give Hoggie a handsome financial reward for arranging with Mr. Lucas to take the message to Mrs. Dawes, and she must do something for Mr. Lucas too. 'Oh, I shouldn't worry about him,' Charles said. 'He spends his life cadging; parsons always do.'

Julia had done well to settle with the only applicant who had offered herself, and one thing was certain, Mrs. Dawes wasn't dotty like Cathie. That was something.

Cathie was unhappy. She had formed the erroneous conclusion that she was settled for life; she adored sleeping in a carpeted bedroom that was fit for a lady, having good food and as much as she liked, and she was amazed to find that the arrangement was ending. She loathed the thought of Mrs. Dawes, was rebellious that she should come to Wetherley at all, and determined to do everything she could to get her out again.

'Her w'n't st'p,' she told Julia. 'You'll see, her w'n't st'p, and that's okay.'

'You're to be nice to her, Cathie.'

Next day Henry went over and fetched Mrs. Dawes again, luggage and all. In some trepidation Julia waited to receive her, full of apprehensions and alarm (one never really knew

194

until the new régime started). She prayed that it would be a success. Charles and Griselda had wanted to come over to tea but deliberately she had put them off, much as she wanted to see them. She wished to be entirely unembarrassed in the act of starting Mrs. Dawes in the job, and felt that she must do this alone.

She stood looking out at the dimming evening with the bronze of September on the trees, and the deer—already the rutting season was just ahead—restless in the park beyond. There was an amethyst mist atop the carp-flecked milkiness of the pool. She thought of the rock gardens, she had done much since Daniel had left and she had intended to do so much more, but somehow she had felt ill; not herself; listless and with much of her energy gone. Also that afternoon when she had dug up all those empty whisky bottles had worried her. The memory of Mrs. Marriner's eyes watching her was sharply etched into her mind. *Now you know the secret* was what those eyes had said, wordlessly, yet startlingly clearly.

Julia could not believe that the one who had drunk the whisky had been Daniel. She wouldn't believe it however apparent it seemed to be. It could have been some distant epoch perhaps, after Theresa died when he was unhappy, something he had conquered and overcome. Or it wasn't he at all, which was far more likely.

There had been no sign of any tendency that way in the lives which she and he had spent together and so happily in these the first few months of their marriage. Daniel did not drink more than Charles, though Charles was no abstainer. Besides, he always preferred wine, and tried to make her drink it with him, but she did not care about it. The childish love of soft drinks stayed lastingly with her. She adored ginger beer.

'To think that I have married a woman who drinks ginger beer!' he had said once, 'what a life it is!'

'I love fizzy drinks.'

'You should try champagne, darling.'

'Ginger beer is nicer,' she had told him and meant it.

He had laughed at the thought, had said one of these days she would grow up and he would change her, and childishly, for no reason at all save that she always spoke before she thought, she had asked, 'Did Theresa like ginger beer?'

He had stared at her almost aghast, as if he could not believe what she had asked him, as if he could never reply, then turned away, his dark eyes with that barricade in them, his throat moving, but saying nothing at all.

She must forget that.

Daniel did not drink spirits, she kept telling herself, and she never alluded to it again.

As she stood awaiting the car to bring Mrs.

Dawes from Penshurst she realized that Mrs. Marriner had deliberately tried to hurt her. From the beginning she had never helped at all. She ran the house well, she cooked beautifully, but about her there had always been the look of a gaoler rather than that of a servant; someone who ruled and was not prepared to do anything else. It was a good thing that the woman had gone. She was deeply in love with Daniel, that was obvious now when she looked back, and Julia tried to thrust it right out of her mind.

She could see Henry bringing the car up the drive between the trees, rounding the corner and turning to the side door. He got out, unloading the boot, and brought two heavy trunks into the house. Julia went round to the door and opened it herself. Mrs. Dawes was standing there looking limp, emotionally constrained, someone vague and perplexed. It was the same brown coat that fitted so badly, no hat, and the eyes were peering from behind the dark glasses that she always had to wear. About her was a sense of forlornness. Of something that was not true.

'So here you are!' Julia said.

'Good afternoon, madam.'

'Henry will take your things up to your room, but you look tired. There is some tea awaiting you in your own little sitting-room. Have it now.'

She had made Cathie prepare tea there.

197

'Thank you,' said Mrs. Dawes.

They went towards the sitting-room together. 'You look troubled,' said Julia kindly, 'tired, would you like a little rest?'

'I have had rather a trying time, madam. I hadn't intended to tell you but something— something unpleasant happened today, my purse was stolen from me.'

'Your purse? Was there much money in it?'

'Quite a lot of money, madam. My wages. And of course it has run me close, very close indeed. I—I don't know how I shall manage.' She clasped hold of the back of a chair, and clung to it so that Julia felt she was ill.

'I can easily advance you something,' she said, 'I don't think there is any need to be so worried because I can see you through.'

'It's very good of you, madam. It's never happened to me before, perhaps that's why it has upset me so much. These days one meets such very strange people.'

'You sit down and have your tea, then I'll show you your room. I don't think there is the least need to worry. I shall leave the dinner to you, you can cook whatever gives you the least trouble for the first evening. There are some cutlets and a chicken in the fridge. I think you'll find that everything is to hand, I only hope it won't be too much for you to do,' and she moved towards the door.

But Mrs. Dawes was not settling down.

'It seems dreadful to worry you, when I have only just come, I mean, but if you lend me a few pounds, it would be a very great favour,' she said for she had returned to the personal worry.

Julia was rather surprised. A few pounds! What did she expect to get? The woman had been in the house only a very few minutes before the story of the stolen purse had been told, and now she had gone back to the offer of a loan. Julia opened her bag and took out three pound notes, aware as she handed them over of a sense of disappointment at the smallness of the amount.

To cover the embarrassment she said, 'You won't really be needing much money here, for everything is supplied, isn't it? Now when you have finished your tea you will find me in the library, it's that door just across the hall. Don't hurry. That's where I shall be.'

'Thank you very much, madam, I'm grateful. It was rather an awful thing to have happen, and I still can't think how it came about, but there one is.'

She was a long time over her tea, before she came to the library. She looked more rested, spoke more quietly, and Julia took her up to the room with the flowers Cathie had put in it. It was a good room looking out across the park to the distant copse at the head of the far lake. An oak tree afflicted with staghead stood gauntly on a mound half-way into the distance, like a cluster of monumental deer gathered together. The bare antlered branches stretched out to right and left against the afternoon sky.

Julia found it difficult to be warm to strangers because she herself was so shy. Until recently she had only met people whom she already knew, with the result that she always suspected those who were unfamiliar, something she could not cure. It was plain that Mrs. Dawes had had a bad time but all that Julia could hope was that she would prove efficient.

When she came into the library where Julia awaited her, Mrs. Dawes had changed into a grey silky dress, one that fitted, and she wore a small muslin apron on it. The smoked glasses were still there, plainly she could not do without them. She asked sensible questions about the dinner and when she was satisfied with the answers went off to the kitchen. Sharp at half-past seven the gong rang, and coming into the hall Julia found that everything was perfect save that the meal had been laid in the big dining-room. It seemed peculiar. She had particularly said that they did not use this room.

Mrs. Dawes listened mutely, then said, 'I'll remember in future.'

She had found where things were, she had common sense, and the table was beautifully laid. The food awaiting Julia was well cooked, in fact she enjoyed it, and after coffee she went to bed early because she felt worn out. She had

200

tired herself with apprehension, grossly exaggerating everything when there had been no need for it, and she would be better for a long night's rest. A hot drink was brought in for her before she finally went to bed. The glass stood on a polished silver salver that Julia had never seen before, and this was set beside her. Obviously it had been a wedding present from the past, and across it was engraved:

Daniel and Theresa
from
Doady

in a man's bold handwriting.

She said: 'I do hope you are not finding things too difficult, Mrs. Dawes?'

'Oh no, madam. I am not afraid of work and I am sure tomorrow the daily women will be helpful.'

'Mrs. Forbes does the cleaning-up before breakfast and gets here very punctually. Cathie has helped tonight?'

'Yes, madam.'

'Poor Cathie! I'm afraid she is—a little—'

'Yes, madam,' and Mrs. Dawes moved to the door. 'Is there anything more you will be wanting, madam?'

Shades of Mrs. Marriner! she thought, and wondered what had happened to her and where she was. 'No, nothing more, thank you,' she said.

She locked her bedroom door that night not knowing why. Falling into a heavy sleep just before dawn she woke to the sound of the early morning tea being set down on the corridor table.

'Your tea, madam,' said a strange voice.

Clumsy with sleep, Julia went to the door to get the tea, and brought in the tray to the bed. There were three letters lying on it. One was from Daniel and she reserved this for the last for it would be a thrill. There was a bill, and another letter which instantly set her trembling for it was the writing she had seen the midnight before her wedding day. I won't open it, she said with courage. But that mood did not last, the letter frightened her too much to stay as it was and of course she did open it. The contents were brief.

Madam,

I left a small suitcase behind me and would be glad if it could be forwarded to the above address, for which I enclose a postal order to cover the expense. I hope you are now satisfactorily suited.

Yours truly,

Marion Marriner.

Julia thought how foolish she had been to be so sickly afraid. Sometimes her weakness

202

alarmed her, even if it was just that flagrant fear of shy youth. She drank the tea, read Daniel's letter, and realized that she felt happier and more relieved than she had done for many days. It was a joy that Mrs. Dawes was established. She would go over to the village and see Charles and Griselda, stay to lunch if she could, and give Mrs. Dawes the opportunity to settle herself here.

It was one of those radiant days which September often brings, and she drove over through exquisite countryside, tawny with the lateness of the year. As she walked up the crazy path that she had laid herself, she could hear Hoggie in the cottage, and she was singing the right hymn. That was something. It was Griselda who came to the door.

'How ill you look!' she said, 'whatever have you been doing to yourself, Julia?'

'I'm feeling wonderful because at last I've got that housekeeper. If Cathie had lived in any longer, it would have killed me, although she is so amiable.'

'The housekeeper is not fierce like Mrs. Marriner?'

'Oh no. She is rather quiet. Vague, I should have thought. Doesn't say much. Maybe it is Wetherley that does that for people, everyone who gets connected with the place seems to be the reserved kind. It doesn't make sense. But don't let's talk about that. I've had a letter from

Daniel and he's coming home next week.'

'Good! Charles will like that, too. He's in the studio. That Mrs. Tanner sent him a frightful letter and he is trying to get the background a bit better because she is coming over to see it this afternoon.'

Julia crossed the strip of back garden bordered in profusion with purple and pink asters, and she went to the barn, Griselda following her. Charles was standing with his back to them, the crumpled blue smock so faded and stained as to be one great smudge. The canvas had a violent new background which he had started only an hour before, acting on one of those impulses which often before had betrayed him. He turned, and seeing Julia burst into a volley.

'You should just see the letter that woman has sent me! You'd have thought if she had her face and wanted a portrait done she couldn't have afforded to be so insulting.'

'There's been a big delay, Charles.'

'If you ask me she's lucky to get anyone to paint her at all. Coming over here this afternoon, too. Charming, isn't it?' He dabbed again at the background.

'I think the alterations are better, Charles.'

'I got the idea of putting in the seven beastly oaks; she might find that theme fascinating, don't you think? But I have never been awfully good at painting oak trees. As to her face, God was ag'in me in that one.'

Julia poised herself on the table edge. 'Has Mrs. Tanner paid yet?'

'Paid? Good Lord, no! Money is what I'm after.'

'But Charles, you have had the Baroness's cheque, that was a fat one, there must be some of it left.'

He shrugged his big shoulders like a boy remembering the sweets he has already eaten. 'What is a mere thousand pounds, Julie darling? It goes so soon and I had debts. Then the new bank manager is a positive glutton for money. The trouble with the man is he doesn't know when he is well off; nothing could be safer than my overdraft, the damned fool! Coming home has been tricky, I thought with Griselda's *dot* I was well off, but things have been happening.'

'The *dot* is Griselda's surely?'

'I told the bank manager that, thinking it was an insurance policy on any little difficulties I had myself. He doesn't take it that way, the fool!' Charles slashed paint on to an oak tree. 'And this has sent me into the arms of our Mrs. Tanner with the pork pie complex, curse the cards.'

It looked as if he was back where he started, Julia thought, but it was good to see him at his easel; he had been away too long.

Half an hour later he came into the house for a picnic lunch. They ate with the doors and

205

windows wide open and the September day creeping into the room with them, all gold and glorious. Charles ate chicken bones with his fingers, reached across and kissed Griselda (because she was so pretty), then drank to the future of Gertie Dawes—God, what a name!—in good English beer. He insisted that Julia must stay and see him through the crisis of the afternoon, because privately he hated the thought though knew it had to be. He detested Mrs. Tanner but he had to get the money from someone, and the thought of the bank manager spurred him on.

Mrs. Tanner arrived an hour before she was expected or wanted. She appeared in a high-standing ancient Rolls driven by a shaggy man in sports coat and a chauffeur's cap, light grey flannels and ginger suède shoes. They saw her coming past the gate in her too-tight navy suit with sables dangling at her throat and a dark blue velvet toque like a church hassock on her head. They spotted her from the studio and a moment later Hoggie came across to tell them that she was here.

'You go and cool her down, Julia,' he said.

'All right.'

When she got to the sitting-room Mrs. Tanner was reposing in a large chair and playing carelessly with a sable tail. She looked up, saw who it was and then said, 'So it's you! I thought you got married?'

'I am married but I came over to see my father.'

'He got married too, didn't he?'

'Yes, we're all awfully happy.' It was something that she had to say. 'He won't be a moment.'

Mrs. Tanner began to talk. She wanted the portrait finished immediately so that it could go to Burlington House for the summer exhibition. It could be done, she was sure.

'It might be a bit difficult,' murmured Julia, well aware that Charles had been outspoken about one of the exhibitions and the taste of the selection committee, which had hardly done him any good.

'I insist on it,' said Mrs. Tanner, 'it is only a matter of knowing the right people and your father must know all the right people.'

Julia could hardly explain that if he did know the right people he had said the most frightful things about them and they were not entirely on his side, as a result. 'I am sure that he will do his best,' she said, and as an afterthought, 'anyway the portrait looks quite beautiful.'

'That's more than it did the last time I saw it,' snapped Mrs. Tanner, 'and I am insistent that it is to go into the Academy. I have already told my friends that it has been accepted so it has got to go there.'

'Naturally,' said Julia, but with alarm.

From the window they could see Charles

approaching, and by the look of him he was not pleased with life. Although he had sincerely hoped to see the last of this woman, he had no wish to see the last of her cheque, and she still owed him the final instalment. What a curse money was! He was for ever up in the clouds and spending lavishly, or down in the dumps with that beastly bank manager ringing him up and being rude, and he with no clue to the answer. He needed her money badly. He came in as though nothing in the world was wrong, and he was boisterously gay. 'You're going to like your picture, Mrs. Tanner,' he said, 'it's got power. It's something and the whole world will dote on it.'

Although Mrs. Tanner knew that she could not trust Charles, and that she wanted to hit him, he had that way with him which could sweep her right off her feet. It swept other people too. He kissed her hand as though he were an Austrian baron, he smiled flatteringly. His hands lifted her from the chair and he suggested that together they should go and look at the picture which had power. He resented her statement about the urgent necessity for an Academy acceptance. What was the Academy anyway? he asked. They went out to the studio.

Griselda had begun to laugh. She thought it was all very funny, but Julia was upset by it and she couldn't laugh.

She said, 'In another five minutes there is

208

going to be one of those appalling rows that do blow up in Charles's studio, and I'm going straight back to Wetherley. I've stayed away too long already and Mrs. Dawes may want me. It is her first day after all, and I'm going back to her.'

She walked out.

★   ★   ★

The drive home took time.

The day was slipping into that somnolent amethyst which always spells autumn. Guildford was in a haze out of which the cathedral stood like a block on the hillside. She turned for home and as she entered the gates of the park and felt the soft scrunch of gravel beneath the wheels, she saw Cathie coming towards her. She was moving in that absurd half-run of hers, her left arm (the deformed one) moving with every step as a bird moves with a broken wing. She waved her good arm at the car and Julia stopped. Cathie came to her side; her face was sweaty, her wispy hair more of a bird's nest than before, and her eyes half bewildered.

'Her 'ent no go'd,' she said.

'What are you talking about, Cathie? Do you mean Mrs. Dawes?'

'Yes. Her 'ent no go'd, she asks me th'ngs. I said I'd tell you. She asked 'bout the m'ster. Where the m'ster is, and th't.'

209

'Of course she wants to know where the master is, and now I'll tell you something. He'll be back next week.'

'She's f'nny,' said Cathie, 'ever so f'nny.'

'Well, you leave it at that,' and Julia drove deliberately on.

She had the curious feeling of limpness, as though she had rounded one tumultuous corner only to find that there was another one ahead, something that she dreaded. She thought of the anonymous letter, the girl called Theresa, and, for no reason, the pile of whisky bottles she had unearthed that hot day when she was gardening. Had they been Mrs. Marriner's? That could have been possible and would explain much. A little tired, she felt that everything would right itself for so soon now Daniel would be home. Things had turned out better in Sweden than he had expected only a few days ago, and she wished that the domestic problem would clear as easily. She'd get used to Mrs. Dawes, of course, but for the moment it worried her. She hated strangers. Possibly that was the bedrock of the whole thing.

She got out of the car and walked into the house, entering the hall just as the telephone bell blared. She took up the receiver. 'Yes?' she said.

It was Clare's voice at the other end.

'I'm back home, Julia. I came rather unexpectedly because things went wrong and I thought it would be far better for everyone if I returned. I suppose I couldn't sup with you tonight? There's no food in the house, and it would be such a help if I could.'

'Of course you can,' but she had this horrid underlying feeling of uneasiness. 'What went wrong?'

'I'll tell you all about it. Half past seven is the right time, isn't it?'

'Yes. I'll see you then.' Julie set down the receiver knowing quite well that somehow she did not want Clare here. She had wished to be alone, but there had been no way of saying so. She saw Mrs. Dawes crossing the far end of the hall and called to her. 'Mrs. Dawes, I am sorry but there is one extra person for dinner. Make no difference in the menu because that will be all right.'

'Thank you, madam.'

Mrs. Dawes had come to the hall table where Julia was standing and she set down a newly cleaned cigarette box on it. The hand that held the box was withered; it was flecked with those brown smudges which are larger than freckles and come so often when the skin is that of a red-head. Yet Gertie Dawes gave no impression of ever having had red hair. The smudges blurred, a darkness which never faded, not born of the sun, but of the skin that could not bear the sun.

Julia said nothing.

She went upstairs, exhausted. She changed

her dress because she always felt that Clare was traditional and of the age before the war when one expected to change in the evenings. She came downstairs again just as the hall door opened and Clare walked in. She looked very sunburnt, and far better than she had done for some time, for undoubtedly the holiday had done her good.

'Hello, Julia!'

'Hello, Clare! Come into the library and have a sherry.'

They went into the library together. Clare was in a good mood, quite talkative, and she had lots to tell of her holiday, the people she had met, and the places she had visited. She was almost warm. She had decided against having pigsties, which Julia knew would please Daniel who had hated the idea from the first. Clare had new plans for her future and thought that it would be much simpler to grow fruit.

'I thought you hated that sort of thing? You had all those apple trees cut down?'

'They were so old, the blossom was their only attribute, and nobody grows apple trees just for the blossom. Livestock asks too much in maintenance, and it is too costly today which is where the profit goes. You don't have to feed fruit that way.'

Julia was thinking of the Weald of Kent in cherry time; the orchards with the scarlet fruit dangling between green spades of leaves; the sound of the men firing guns to alarm marauding birds. Later in the year too, when those first red apples came, and on either side of the road the apple orchards gave the first touch of autumn to the scene.

'I'd rather do fruit,' Clare was saying. 'I think it is so awful when the pigs are killed. I suppose that goes for chickens too, and it *is* quite horrible, yet one never minds picking the fruit.'

'I think Daniel would help you with trees.'

The evening had died young; now the nights were closing in rapidly, each one noticeably shorter than its predecessor. Tonight through the library window they could see the view across to the Hog's Back, and a brilliant clear young moon which had already risen. Clare was eagerly talking of the apples, perhaps Daniel had been right when he had said that pigs would smell, perhaps they were difficult and the bottom was dropping out of the market.

The gong rang a little before its time, and when they went into the small dining-room the soup was on the table, and Mrs. Dawes had already returned to the kitchen.

Clare said, 'It's odd Mrs. Marriner suddenly taking offence and clearing off like she did. I always felt I liked her.'

'She didn't like me,' said Julia.

Clare nodded. 'Oh well, I suppose she was half in love with Daniel. In her own funny way of course. He had been awfully good to her, and perhaps she thought she could land him with her *soufflés* and tipsy cake. It has caught men before now. How did you get hold of this new woman? People tell me it isn't as easy as it once was.'

Sitting at the head of the table Julia explained the difficulties. She had been horrified to find herself all alone in the big house, and after that at the mercies of Cathie. She had heard of Mrs. Dawes through the local parson, and through Hoggie.

'I was at my wits' end when it happened. I got her to come for an interview, she seemed shy, rather offhand, I thought, but I've got the idea that Wetherley does that to people. Mrs. Marriner was like it, too.'

'But she had had such a ghastly time in Holland, I do understand how she may have felt.'

'Perhaps she should have left when I came here.'

'Only that people never do such a thing,' said Clare slowly.

Julia did not pursue the subject but pressed the electric bell on the table. 'You'll see Mrs. Dawes. For heaven's sake don't say anything that may make her take umbrage.' She pushed back the thick hair from her eyes with hands grown tired. She seemed to tire so easily just now. She poured out the last of her ginger beer. 'I couldn't bear it if this woman left and I had to get Cathie back in the house.'

'I'll not say a word however badly I feel.'

The door opened and Mrs. Dawes came in. She wore the grey silk dress and the little apron; the smoked glasses gave her face a remote expression, and the scar across her cheek showed tonight more than usual. It was withered and puckered so that the mouth, high on one side, dropped at the other corner. It was shocking to think that any woman's face could be so humiliated.

She set a tray on the side, came for the soup plates saying nothing, and she moved quietly, then she took the tray away. Julia knew that Clare was closely watching her.

As the door shut, she asked, 'Well?'

'There's something about her that makes me feel I have seen her somewhere before. I can't think where. What has happened to her face?'

'Apparently she had a bad car accident.'

'It must have been a pretty ghastly one. Poor thing! I think it was her hands that struck a memory with me. I see such lots of people on committees and things, for the world is a mass of refugees and displaced persons, out-of-works and down-and-outs, that I get a bit mixed.' She reached for more toast and began to butter it, yet not looking at Julia.

Mrs. Dawes brought in the chicken and the vegetables. She carved beautifully on the side, her back to them, and Julia went on with an almost agitated run of conversation to hide anything that might be wrong. The plates came to the table, the vegetables were served. Mrs. Dawes went away again.

'Do you remember her?' asked Julia, surprisingly interested.

'No. No, I don't. She is just someone I have seen, I suppose, I don't know where, I don't know when.'

'I hope she isn't another of your displaced persons. Mrs. Marriner was bad enough.'

'Anyway this woman could not attract Daniel, could she? When Mrs. Marriner first came here she was very pretty.'

'Not really?'

'Oh yes she was. That was in Theresa's time, and she was very pretty. Theresa liked her, I remember; I could never think why, but she trusted her. She was like that,' and she paused.

'Tell me about Theresa?' Julia asked. 'I know nothing, and I...' She was avid for information.

'Oh no, I'd better not do that. Daniel wouldn't like it, and after all he does give me an allowance.'

Hush money, Julia thought, and was ashamed of herself for thinking it. She was embarrassed with herself for putting it that way, yet nothing was more natural than for her to want to know about the first wife, the girl with the violet eyes that searched her from the canvas whenever she

216

came into this room.

The telephone rang.

Julia got up. 'Oh dear, I'll have to go and answer it. Clare, when you've done do ring for the sweet, will you? It's a *soufflé*, and if I'm a long time it'll spoil.' She went into the hall and picked up the receiver; Charles spoke from the other end.

He said, 'Julia? Thank God it's you. There's a crisis here, Griselda thinks she's going to have a baby.'

'Surely that's a bit sudden?' They had parted but a few hours before and she could not imagine what had happened.

'That Tanner woman said so. Says she knows by the eyes, and Griselda is for it all right. She has been a bit worried for some days and never said a thing, now this has finished it. Can I bring her over to see you? She's quite hysterical.'

'Clare is here with me. She came unexpectedly, had no food in the house and is supping here.'

'Well, you can get rid of old sour-puss surely? We don't want her in a *cause intime* like this one.'

'I can hardly ask her to go.'

'I don't see why not. I should. Get rid of her for God's sake, for this is the devil.'

'I can't believe it's true.'

'It isn't going to be true, you can take that from me!' said Charles with his old spirit, 'but that's that. Get rid of her and we'll be with you in a moment.'

'Yes,' said Julia reluctantly and he rung off.

She had not thought of a step-brother or sister, and that idea in itself was something of a shock. Charles would go dotty with a baby. She walked slowly back to the dining-room, half dazed by the crisis. She could hear Clare and Mrs. Dawes talking in low voices, probably Clare was making herself pleasant or had found out where they had met before. As Julie entered, the woman turned from the side table and went out of the room. Clare was sitting there not eating, and looking very pale. She also looked dazed, Julia thought, but that was possibly because she herself was feeling so peculiar that she exaggerated things. She sat down.

'There is something of a panic at home. Charles is bringing Griselda over here the moment they can manage it.'

'Is he?'

'He—he wants a private talk.' Julia knew that she was putting this badly, but what else could she do? Usually Clare was tardy at taking a hint, it had not occurred to Julia that she would understand and make it easy for her with startling suddenness, but she did.

'You'd like to be alone then, of course. I'll go back to the Dower House the moment we've finished dinner.'

218

'It sounds as if I were turning you out, Clare, and I don't want that.'

'Not at all. I'm tired from the journey, anyway,' She did look tired, almost haggard, though Julia had not noticed it until Clare had drawn her attention to it. 'An early bed would be an idea.' She paused, her eyes far away. Then she said, 'You won't want to walk across the park with me, but you know the deer have always made me nervous. Could Mrs. Dawes come, do you think?'

'If she isn't afraid of the dark and the deer.'

'I'll run and ask her.' Clare did not wait for Julia's reply but went straight off. If she had not been so concerned about Charles's news, probably Julia would have realized that something was wrong here, but she didn't. He would arrive in an uproar. He would probably fly off to Austria to tell the Baroness the news, and there would be one of his enormous fusses.

Coffee had to be hurried. Julia was absent-minded, Clare restless, and she had gone quiet. Obviously she wanted to get away before Charles arrived, and she did not stay. She herself took the tray out to Mrs. Dawes and asked if the washing-up was almost done. It was. Mrs. Dawes was a very quick person, and a few moments later she came for Clare with the big tweed coat pulled shapelessly over her shoulders. It hung on her wretched thinness in bags, like a coat on a hook, not on a woman at

219

all.

'Are you sure you don't mind going?' Julia asked her.

'Not at all, madam. I'm used to country life, and the dark and the deer mean nothing to me.'

Clare watched her; she was blinking like some owl confused by daylight. Every little while that mauve tongue moistened her thin lips and she swallowed hard. 'Something's frightened her,' Julia thought, 'but there is no time for bothering about that now.' She went to the door to wave them away. They went off together with an electric torch. 'I wonder what has upset her?' Julia asked herself.

★   ★   ★

Julia came back into the library feeling limp and exhausted, not because Charles thought there would be a child but because this was the way she herself felt. She had been feeling so ill recently, the tiredness which came when she should not have been tired and which worried her; the sickness which was surely more than her childhood's bilious attacks, certainly it came more frequently.

Each morning, or almost each morning, she woke with it, and despaired of it getting better. She thought quite suddenly, 'Supposing *I* am going to have a baby?' For a moment she shrank before it, as every woman does before she and

220

the child within her become known to each other. Then as it seemed to be a prediction taking form in her heart, it changed, for a new inspiration seemed to infuse her. This would be the fulfilment of her love for Daniel; it would be the heir that Theresa had never given him, the child he once had said he would love to possess.

She got up feeling elated. She went into the hall for now it did not matter that she had been so alone in the house; with her child she was no longer alone. She went into the big dining-room, for that was where she wanted to be.

She switched on the light and instantly the great crystal chandelier sprang into full radiance, a quivering, glistening mass of diamonds. The walls and curtains had the greyness of autumnal mists, and over the pink marble mantelpiece the light lit the face of Theresa, and it turned to look at her. Theresa was so young, so gay, so beautiful with the red hair which was much the same colour as the tawny beech leaves behind her; her eyes were so violet. She laughed at Julia. 'Theresa was too lovely to die,' she thought tragically, 'and she must have had so much to live for.'

She went closer to the picture. It was a beautiful piece of work and Charles admired its genius. Theresa's eyes followed her until she stood before it, then they looked away into the distance. *I am here*, was what those eyes said. *I am still beautiful. If I never had a child I was*

221

Daniel's first love, I was his first wife . . .

Julia heard the violent ringing of the doorbell and knew that Charles had already arrived and was madly impatient. She ran to greet him.

CHAPTER TEN

'THIS is a nice to-do!' said Charles marching into the house in front of Griselda. He wore an enormous teddy-bear coat that he had bought in pre-war days and was much too small for him, but kept him warm. It had a hoop at the back, which looked grotesque, where he had sat too long in it. His red hair was unbrushed, his face crimson. 'I can tell you, Julie, when I got wind of this it shot me sky-high.'

Griselda came in saying nothing; she was pale, her face pinched, and her eyes quite dark with fear.

'Look here,' said Julia, 'let's take it quietly. Come along and have a whisky and soda first, Charles.'

'And how!'

Griselda followed them into the library and sank down forlornly on the sofa there. Julia knew that there was a common bond between them, for she also was going to have a child. Nobody knew yet; it was a secret between herself and one other, someone whom as yet she did not know, yet knew completely. She went over to the tray of drinks that Mrs. Dawes had prepared for this moment, and she picked up the whisky decanter. It was light, almost empty.

'Whatever's happened here?' she asked herself. 'Could it have sprung a leak?' and aloud, 'Wait a moment, Charles, I must get another bottle.' She dived into the cupboard where Daniel kept his secret store and to which she and she alone had the key. Two bottles stood there, the thin white paper covering from the shop about them. She thought quite clearly, 'There should have been four,' and was perplexed. Perhaps this was being one of those muddling evenings in which she made mistakes. They seemed to be crowding in on her. There was little point in worrying about a couple of bottles of whisky now when other and far more important crises were offering themselves.

'Here we are,' she said.

Charles came straight to the point, his face puckered with agitation. 'Whatever happens I simply can't let this thing be. I'm far too old. Let's have courage and face the bitter truth. I've put things of youth behind me, and I'd look a dam' fool playing "Pat-a-cake, pat-a-cake, baker's man" at my age.'

'But Charles, you aren't too old.'

'That's what you think!' He lifted his glass and pulled a wry face at it. '*Slanti,* and all that stuff!'

He gulped down a mouthful.

Griselda started talking, very slowly indeed. 'I am one of those people who have always been afraid of having a baby.'

'Don't let that worry you, because you aren't going to have a baby, whatever you think,' said Charles brightly. 'The world is full of resourceful doctors who have moral principles about women who are afraid of having babies.'

'But I'm frightened of that sort of thing, too.'

'There's nothing to it, I believe,' said Charles with exaggerated carelessness. 'You go into hospital and have your appendix out; nobody minds losing an appendix because it doesn't mean a thing. No good to you, only rabbits find them useful, and God knows what they do with them. Don't worry, my darling, I shan't let anybody hurt you.'

Julia spoke very gently. 'If Griselda is frightened, you aren't making it any better for her, so do shut up, Charles. Drink down your whisky and then let's talk.'

'*Müttchen* would like an heir,' commented Griselda, weighing up the pros and cons.

'Then let *Müttchen* dam' well have it!' said Charles crossly. 'Babies mean bad nights, teething troubles, and in the end the little basket grows up into a brute of a Teddy who flays the hide off poor old ladies who can't defend themselves. By all means let *Müttchen* have it!'

'She's too old.'

The remark seemed to inflame Charles's sense of injustice, for he turned angry. 'That's where that old bitch Nature helps women. She gives them the get-out, and never does the same for a chap like me. If I were your *Müttchen*, at my age I couldn't; but because I'm me, I can, and seem to have done it. Isn't it hell?'

Charles was one of those reckless happy-go-luckies who live today for today and let tomorrow go its own way. Julia tried to get things sorted out. 'Whilst you are making all this fuss, are you sure? I mean, has Griselda seen a doctor?'

'No. She's quite convinced. What I now intend to do is to fly back to Austria, and see Professor Streiswasser.'

'Oh, but Charles, you keep buzzing to and fro, and it is so absurd. And so expensive. Why not see Dr. Middleton? After all, so far it is only guesswork and I don't believe it's true. The village women like that had that far-away look in their eyes. Cats get it, too. I've noticed it.'

'If tom-cats get it, then it's mine!' said Charles with gloom, but Julia knew that already she had cheered him though he was in the mood that would not admit it. 'No, she hasn't that far-away look. I wonder if it was the pie we had for lunch.'

Griselda broke down.

In the present situation she was just a little girl again. When they had comforted her there

225

was the sound of Mrs. Dawes returning, and Julia rang for hot coffee to console Griselda, and Mrs. Dawes brought it in. Julia did not know why yet again she thought of the empty whisky decanter; she was almost sure it had been half full at lunch, but did not relish asking about it lest the woman took offence. It could have been Cathie, or Mrs. Forbes, or Mrs. Bentley, but it was odd that they had never done it before. With three other people in the house she realized the folly of committing herself. Until Daniel's return Mrs. Dawes must stay here at all costs, she had made up her mind to that.

Griselda was now consoled. 'You are a darling, Julie. I want a baby, of course, but not just now and not this one.'

'I don't want a baby,' said Charles, helping himself to another whisky. 'If you had had Julie cutting that blasted last double tooth of hers, you wouldn't want it either! Night after night of solid hell, and the neighbours complaining to add to it. No, I could never repeat that.'

Julia said: 'I apologize. But I do suggest that you see Dr. Middleton. He's awfully nice and it would be something to make quite sure before you let yourselves get all fussed.'

This enchanted Charles.

There was no point in mentioning her own anxieties when Charles and Griselda were so worried about their problem. They sat on talking, every hour growing brighter, and it was after midnight when they left, Charles now gaily exuberant. He thought they had jumped the gun! They'd get an appointment with Dr. Middleton tomorrow, which was already today.

Julia waved them from the door, and when the car had driven off she waited to hear it going down the drive, and gradually the sound fading into the distance; then she came inside again, and bolted the door behind her. She went upstairs and reached for the switch at the head to turn out the light below. Happening to glance down she saw that Mrs. Dawes had come out of the lighted kitchen and was standing in the hall looking up at her. She was ghost-like. Perhaps there WAS something of the phantom about her.

Julia spoke involuntarily. 'Oh dear, I nearly switched off the light; I had no idea you were still up and I'm sorry. Good night.'

'Good night, madam.'

No more.

Julia felt that there should have been more. She went into her room on edge. She was being awfully silly.

Late the following afternoon Charles rang up in a fit of joy, for they had seen Dr. Middleton. There was nothing in last night's pandemonium, and in his present excitement he could not think how he had got the wind-up so badly. He was so elated that he had put the final touches to Mrs. Tanner's portrait and now she would have to pay for it whatever happened.

Julia was actually laughing when he had done.

She went into the library for her tea, sitting over the fire, for it was a dull day and already the thought of a fire towards evening was pleasant. There comes a moment when summer dies and one turns to the hearth-side again to find it welcoming.

Mrs. Dawes brought in a letter on the silver salver with *Daniel and Theresa* sprawled across it. Glancing at the writing on the envelope, Julia saw that it was from Clare. It was most unusual for them to write to each other, and she could not understand why Clare had written now.

Dear Julia,

I have been thinking it over and I am sure that I have seen Gertrude Dawes before, as I said. Please keep this to yourself; I don't want her to know that I have mentioned it to you, but I do think you should be rid of her. Don't ring me up about it, please; in any case I am leaving home tonight for a week, but I wanted you to think this over. She is not the right person for you, and even Cathie Hawkes sleeping in the house would be better.

Forgive haste, and do please think about this.

As ever,
Clare.

It was one of the most extraordinary letters that Julia had ever received. She could not imagine why it was that Clare did not tell her why she was worried; the two of them had walked across the park the night before; had something transpired then? Something that Clare did not like to admit? Couldn't she have told Julia what it was? Now she was intensely uneasy. But one thing she did not agree to was that Cathie would be a wiser project. Clare had not had Cathie in the house with her and did not know how awful she was. In another week Daniel would be returning home and she could wait until then. At the same time she had broken into a nervous sweat.

She went up to her room and bathed her face. She took a bottle of eau-de-Cologne and sprayed her throat and arms; it was refreshing. Suddenly she got the idea that whilst she did it someone had tried the door handle, very gently, with hardly any sound to it, and then had withdrawn her hold again. She wheeled round sharply to find no one there. She had got herself absurdly worked-up, of course, and it was ridiculous.

Nothing had happened.

Nothing at all.

She sat for a while on the dressing-stool watching the door reflected in the triple mirror before her, and still convinced that someone would open it and come in to speak to her. Someone she did not want to see. Then she heard Cathie at the run going down the corridor and humming a hymn tune to herself, which was another little trait of hers.

Then she opened the door herself and went downstairs, but worn out with sheer panic.

Next day she breakfasted late with that dreadful unrefreshed feeling of someone who has not slept properly. She told herself that she must be more reasonable; there had been nothing to be afraid of last night, only in her own imagination and she must quench that. Perhaps it was that she had allowed circumstances to take possession of her, and was exaggerating everything. When she went downstairs the house was dead ordinary. After all there was nothing ominous about the fact that the house-keeper had watched her as she went upstairs, probably only to see if she put the light out or forgot it.

Mrs. Dawes brought in the coffee. 'Good morning, madam,' she said.

'Good morning. I'm late, I am afraid, but I haven't been feeling at all well again. It's this wretched biliousness. I shall go and see the doctor and get something for it; there is no point in letting it go on.'

She glossed over it, because at no cost could she admit the truth, certainly not to this woman.

'No, madam.'

Perhaps she had arrived at the point when everything that Mrs. Dawes did or said made her suspicious. Her senses were sharpened by doubt. All the time she was defensive. Why should Clare have been so sure that Mrs. Dawes was not the right person to be here, that even Cathie would be better? Again Julia thought of the empty decanter. Who ever was taking it it could not be Cathie, for the one sterling point about her was that she was dead honest. Mrs. Bentley or Mrs. Forbes would have done it before now, and with that certain fact she could rule both of them out. Which left only Mrs. Dawes!

Perhaps the doctor could help her, make her more sure of herself and change everything.

After lunch she went to see him.

★   ★   ★

The day had cleared.

A fickle sun was trying to dispel the greyness of cloud and mist; it came out in thin yellow between the darkness, and there was promise in it, Julia knew. She was, she realized, going to make certain (though she herself was already sure), and Dr. Middleton would help her.

His was a pleasant house in a mere hamlet just outside Guildford, a hamlet which straggled for about half a mile along the road. He saw her in the friendly consulting-room with little of the National Health atmosphere about it; he always saw private patients at this hour. The wall was soft rose and had faded slightly with an amiable pleasantness, the furniture was chipped, the couch broken in one place, for this room worked

231

hard for its living, as did the man. He was grey-haired, with an encouraging smile, and she knew that she had every confidence in him.

'Well, you're looking peaky, Mrs. Strong.'

'I'm feeling peaky, too.'

He sat down at the desk with a calendar for yesterday before him, a blotter on which he had doodled much, and a half-filled inkpot. He asked her questions and she answered them carefully. He made an examination, running over her with long fingers, and when he had finished set a screen round her and left her to finish dressing whilst he went back to his desk. Eventually she came round the screen with an extraordinary feeling of tiredness about her.

He looked at her. 'It's all right, you know. There's nothing to be the least bit worried about.'

She sat down in the chair. 'The sickness is such a bother and it seems to be getting worse. I hate it. One can faint with decency; being sick is another story,' and she pushed her hair back with that little familiar gesture of hers.

'Our mothers all went through this when we were coming.'

'Meaning...?'

'Yes,' he said, 'that is exactly what I do mean. I should have said next April.'

It would be the very month when she and Daniel had first met, and one of the loveliest of the year. Her mind was back to the night when they had stood on the Clopton Bridge with the faint scent of brackish water, of marigolds and meadowland. Then she had the feeling that the beautiful emotion within her had not lasted for a few hours only but for her whole life, something that she had always wanted. There had been the music of *Mignon*. Today another, an even lovelier, feeling came to her, sweeter than the night with the sound of the Avon lapping the stanchions of a bridge built in 1066, the smell of water and the sweet persuasive sound of music from the boathouse.

'I am so glad,' she said a trifle hoarsely, 'so very glad,' and for a moment she dropped her face into her hands. When she looked up again, she said, 'I think I want a boy.'

'Let's hope it will be a boy. More boys are born than girls, so nature is on your side.'

'It will be a boy,' she said with conviction.

He became entirely practical, telling her what she should do, making out a prescription to cope with the sickness, and helping her with advice. He wished her well, speaking encouragingly more like some amiable middle-aged relative than a doctor, and she went out of the house feeling happier.

What would Charles say about this? What would Griselda say? Most of all, what would Daniel say when he got back? She went into the town to get the prescription made up, and had to wait a little while so that when she got home the afternoon was turning into a dusty grey again.

She went into Wetherley for the tea that was waiting for her in the library, and she flung down her coat on to a chair. Cathie came in. At this moment there was something about Cathie's absurdly gummy smile which was most welcoming.

'Everything all right, Cathie?' she asked.

'Wh'n's M'ster c'ming back?'

'Next week.' A week yesterday, she thought, only six days more, for today had almost gone, and she would have so much to tell him when he returned. Cathie stood looking at her and grinning.

'Okay.' Then, 'His w'sky's go'ng,' she said.

'What do you mean?'

Cathie lurched slightly towards Julia, and nodded with the profound intimacy of the half-wit when she hopes to share a secret. 'Mrs. D'wes,' she said and nodded more vigorously.

'Cathie, you mustn't tell tales.'

'You l'ok at the b'tle, ma'am.'

'Nonsense! You run along,' and playfully she pushed Cathie from her. Cathie began to trot to the door, muttering to herself, then from the door she turned to laugh again and had gone.

Julia looked at the bottle, and it was then that she became quite sure. She stood there with the decanter in her hand and suddenly she thought of those other bottles, the empty ones that she had dug up, and she connected the two. Could it be that there was some horrifying association with whisky here in Wetherley? Was it part of her foolish apprehensions? She couldn't think, because part of her was so afraid. But Daniel would be home soon, then she would have it out with him, she would tell him what had happened and how distressed she was, and he would help her.

She sat over the fire for a time with the paper, she must have dozed for she did not know how fast time had moved on until the gong rang. She went into the little dining-room where the soup was waiting for her. The round two-handled Napoleon ivy soup bowl was set before her, the silver was beautifully polished, and the bowl of cerise asters in the centre charmingly arranged. It looked pretty; it looked secure and was home; how silly it was to get so distraught about it all! When she rang, Mrs. Dawes came in with cutlets in a silver entrée dish. Julia got the feeling that the smell of spirits lingered about her, and knew that once again she was horrified as to what to do next. She finished the cutlets and the light sponge pudding that followed them.

'I'll have coffee in the library,' she said, and tonight she would lock up the whisky so that nobody could touch it. Yet dare she do this? It might arouse resentment. What would she say if Mrs. Dawes challenged her? She realized that

235

she would be far wiser to let things continue as they were, anyway till Daniel got home and could help her. When he was here she would not be so nervous, which would be a comfort.

The telephone rang and when she went to it, it was Charles.

'Well, and how are you?' he asked.

'I've been to see Dr. Middleton myself. You know I told you I was feeling rotten, and what do you think is happening? I'm having a baby in April.'

'What did you say?'

She repeated it with emphasized laboriousness, her eyes laughing.

'Good Lord! Darling, what a thrill! This is the news of the day.' It seemed extraordinary that the information which had so dismayed him with Griselda the day before yesterday, enthralled him with Julia. 'And April, too! What a damned good time of the year to have a birthday, as long as it isn't the first, of course! I must tell Griselda.'

She heard him calling his wife, and when he returned Julia spoke first. 'Charles, I am so excited, and just realize how Daniel will feel! The last three weeks have been rotten, and . . .' she dropped her voice, going quickly to another subject. 'I'm worried to death about this new woman.'

'Gertie Dawes? I thought that name did not bode well, and here it comes! What's she been doing?'

Speaking still lower, because she was so afraid, 'I think she is sneaking the whisky.'

'Well, lock it up!'

'I thought I had locked it up. Only Daniel and I are supposed to have the keys, there are only two of them, but it would almost seem that she knows how to get at it, only of course that isn't possible.'

'Supposing I come over and drink it all for her?' Gaily, for he had gone back to the news of the day, 'I can't imagine myself as a grandfather, of course, and I don't feel like one. I wish the mind did not stay so eternally young, because it is a fat lot of use, but . . .'

'I know,' she said.

'What's the matter? You sound different.'

'Nothing. Just nothing.' Mrs. Dawes had come into the room for the coffee tray; she did not look in Julia's direction, just picked it all up and went out again almost silently. It must be that she was so on edge, Julia thought, for having a baby was a big job, and it made one peculiar about almost everything. She had felt suspicious about Mrs. Marriner, and that fear had grown rapidly, but then she had realized that the woman had actually hated her. She had found that she had written that anonymous letter, and in the end the climax had been inescapable. She knew that.

Charles was chattering. 'We'll come over

tomorrow and have a celebration lunch. I presume old Gertie can cook a decent meal?'

'Not too bad.'

'Then there we are. *Au revoir* till tomorrow. Make it champagne and be damned to the cost!' He rang off.

After Julia had lost the comforting sound of his voice she could not settle to her book again. It no longer held her. At half-past ten Mrs. Dawes would come in to know if she would like hot milk, or Ovaltine, or fruit juice. She dreaded the thought of it, and absurdly so for there was no reason. She kept glancing at the clock, took up knitting and abandoned it, then Patience and abandoned that. On the very stroke of half-past the door opened and here was Mrs. Dawes.

'I wondered if you would like some hot milk tonight, madam?'

'No, thank you. I think a fruit drink.'

'Orange or lemon?'

'Orange will do, please.'

Mrs. Dawes had gone away again, walking very erectly, her body rising up from her thin waist. Her figure was younger than her face but it was possible that her intense thinness gave the impression of youth whereas the wrinkles and the dead colour of her skin made her face seem old. She returned with the tray and on it was a glass of orange juice with small crystal icebergs bobbing in it. She set it down beside Julia.

Julia did not know why she asked it, but the question came quite impulsively. 'Thank you. I believe you and my sister-in-law have met before somewhere? Do you remember?'

'I have met a great many people in my life, madam, you see I have travelled a lot.'

'But you have never been in this part of the world before? Not until you took the job at Penshurst?' For a moment Julia got the idea that the eyes behind the smoked glasses were searching her.

'That is not quite true, I have been here before.'

'Perhaps that was when you met?'

'I was a child at the time, madam.'

Mrs. Dawes must be a good deal older than Clare; Julia had not dared to ask her exact age at the interview, because she felt too young and embarrassed and it had seemed to be a little impertinent. She had stayed discomfited, trying to think of some pleasant phraseology for it, then the conversation had gone on to something else and the opportunity had slipped by. 'Your people lived here?'

'No, madam, my people did not live here, but I came here,' and about her was that vibrant tone almost defiant, something that Julia dared not challenge.

'Near Wetherley, I hope,' she said.

'Not far from Wetherley, and it was only for a very short time.' The tone had changed again as

239

though she had become aware of Julia's suspicion and was more careful. She moved towards the door and as she went Julia spoke again.

'Was the house lovely then? Was the park as beautiful?'

'No, madam, it wasn't,' then in a sudden burst contradicting everything she had just said, her voice ringing with a curious enthusiasm, 'Wetherley was always the loveliest place that I have ever known.'

'It still is,' Julia murmured.

She had gone, and in a strange mood tonight; that last remark had been a vigorous confession of a deep affection for Wetherley, a place she had known since childhood. Perhaps this explained why she had come here so eagerly, remembering a child's joy in it. It had struck Julia as odd that she should take the job on, for there was far too much work for one woman to do alone, and this in spite of the women who came in.

Mrs. Marriner had undertaken it willingly of course, but that was because she was in love with Daniel, and felt there was something she could get out of it, perhaps marriage, and if not marriage his promiscuous love which would be satisfying. But there was nothing this woman could get out of the house.

Nothing at all.

Sitting with the fruit drink Julia realized there

must have been some reason, and the reason was not herself, or the wages, or the job. Could it have been Daniel? She wished that she had asked, 'Did you ever meet my husband here?' but something about Mrs. Dawes' tone had not permitted questions. What she had said conveyed that she had in mind a lovely picture of Wetherley as a child. The smooth undulating parkland with the deer; the shimmering swans on the far lake, white ships travelling between banks of codlings and cream in summer, of daffodils in spring, and of defiant pampas grasses in autumn; the milkiness of the small lake standing as it did before the house, so that on hot summer days the mirrored beauty of a drowned Wetherley lay reflected in it; tonight with early autumn the lake smelt of dank water. Julia had noticed it just before dinner when she had drawn the curtains back to see if there was a halo round the moon. In the silver of starshine and night the park had been a cameo and the stars sheer beauty, the night radiant. But there *had* been a halo round the moon.

She finished the orange drink and got up.

She shook the cushions, which she had always done at home to save Hoggie when she came in the morning, because she was a dear old thing and she had a lot to do. She went on shaking cushions even here, where Cathie would come so early and liked doing them herself. She went to the door and opened it, but timidly this time.

She turned out the light and shut the door behind her.

There was only one bulb burning in the hall, and the place looked dreary, which was unusual, for Wetherley was a bright house. She went upstairs with the library book under her arm, and her heart making silly noises. It is youth, she told herself, youth and my stupid imagination! Nobody is watching me, why should there be? There is no ghost in Wetherley.

She went into her room and locked the door behind her.

Ever since that first lunch on her wedding day in this house she had been impressed by the beauty of this room; the ceiling with its delicate sprays of almond blossom, the mossy carpet, and the soft tenderness of early springtime on the walls. Now the lights were burning screened in pink silk, giving the feeling that the place was warm.

She went over to the electric fire.

In the bed the hot water bottle would be wrapped in her nightdress warming it for her, for Mrs. Dawes was assiduous in her attention. Slowly Julia began to undress. After all, it was one day nearer to seeing Daniel again, and that was something. Night had a comforting way of ironing out the creases, and the door locked she was safe from that unknown fear. Whatever she told herself, the unknown fear was quite ridiculous, it did not matter. The woman whose hand had written her that wretched letter had gone for ever.

Don't marry him. You know nothing about him and you'll only live to regret it.

Perhaps the truth was that she had allowed the situation to get on her nerves; if she had shared the secret with someone in the beginning it would all have been so much easier, but she hadn't done.

Last thing of all she thought 'I didn't lock the whisky away. I meant to do it, and I didn't. How silly I am!'

CHAPTER ELEVEN

AT breakfast as soon as Mrs. Dawes had left Julia with the grilled kidneys and hot coffee she went over to the sideboard to see what had happened to the whisky decanter. She lifted it up so that she could get the light shining through it. It was bone dry.

Then she *is* sneaking it, Julia told herself, and despairingly for she knew she would never have the courage to attack Mrs. Dawes on this. It was quite horrible to be so weak, and so young, and so stupid. Worse to be already so dreadfully afraid of someone.

She wished she had never noticed the loss of the whisky.

She was so panicky that she could not eat her breakfast and was going out into the garden for air, when suddenly she could not remember if she had warned Mrs. Dawes that Charles and Griselda were coming over for lunch. She went across the hall to the kitchen. As she approached, she heard a most disturbing sound. It was a long low sob. The sob was hard, it was bitter in the extreme and intensely pathetic. In Wetherley strange things were always happening, strange *little* things, and Julia felt the old fear.

Opening the kitchen door quickly, she saw that Mrs. Dawes was sitting in the big wooden chair, her face in her hands and weeping bitterly. She was crying so much that she could not have heard the sound of the door opening, and realized Julia was there only by that sixth sense which makes one aware of another presence. She turned to look. It was the first time that Julia had seen her without those smoked glasses that she wore. Her eyes were ugly for she had no lashes. The skin around them was parched and perished, the sockets deep, and in the pale blue of those eyes, faded beyond belief, there was despair. Julia saw the face of what seemed to be quite an old woman, a depraved woman who had tasted fully from

244

life's cup of desire, and having emptied the cup had come to the dregs to find them biting and bitter.

'Oh, Mrs. Dawes, whatever is the matter? Are you ill?' and she asked it with sympathy.

Without hurrying the woman put out an old hand for the dark glasses and set them back into place almost as though she was uneasy without them.

'I have toothache,' she said; both of them knew that it was a lie.

'Do take time off and go and see the dentist. There is a very good one in Frimley, shall I ring him up for you?'

'I'll ring up. I could perhaps go when lunch is over.' Her voice had become controlled again and her sobs stopped. Furtively she lifted her hand and wiped away a large tear that had dripped to the baggy side of her chin and hung there like a miniature icicle.

'We'll have lunch early and that will make it easier for you. My father and stepmother are coming over, but if you are not feeling well don't make too much fuss. There is some cold chicken which will do.'

'Thank you, madam.'

'I had a letter from Sweden this morning. Things are going better after all and my husband may be home sooner than any of us thought. You must be well for his return.'

'Yes, madam.'

245

Julia knew she ought to say more, something sympathetic which would be helpful, but the words would not come. In the end she turned, half ashamed of herself, and went out into the garden.

It was one of those lovely mornings which come when summer is slowly dying. Never had the trees been fuller, or the flowers more imperial in their colours. Banks of lavender michaelmas daisies hedged the flower beds; red hot pokers thrust up triumphantly behind them, and this was a wonderful year for asters. She walked into the rock garden which she had meant to improve so much whilst Daniel was away, but somehow she had not had the energy. Now she knew why. It was nice to think of his return. They would engage another housekeeper, he would know how to help, and she thought that a married couple would be by far the most suitable proposition. She would prefer another man to be here, for Henry the chauffeur lived in the village and only came and went. She wandered into the park smelling freshly of grass, down to the far lake by the swans, and she did not come back until midday, then realizing that the hours had gone fast. Charles's old car was coming up the drive, he and Griselda in it.

Julia walked off the grass verge between the oak trees to meet them. 'Hi there!' she called.

Charles stopped the car quickly, and jumped

out. 'I say, Julia! What news! You kept pretty quiet about it, didn't you? Not that I like the idea of being a grandpapa, I don't suppose anybody does really, but there you are!'

'You didn't want to be a Dad the night before last!'

They crammed into the car, the three of them, and drove on up to the front door. Griselda had brought the first present for the baby, a tiny white teddy bear wrapped in tissue paper, and they laughed about it as they went into the library for drinks. Julia had thrown off her despondent mood, she was gay again and happy. Daniel was returning, she would have a baby, everything was working out the right way.

'I've heard from Daniel; the problem of this and that going wrong is over, and he may be back earlier. It's wonderful, isn't it?'

'Is he thrilled about the baby?' from Griselda.

'He doesn't know a thing yet!'

'Ha! I knew first!' Charles rubbed his hands together like a schoolboy. 'That's something, isn't it? Now then. Here's to the baby,' and he lifted his glass.

'To all of us!' said Griselda.

She wore one of those pouched white blouses of hers, and the full swinging skirt. She looked almost strange in this setting of serene English landscape, yet about her was the infinite charm of Austria.

'You'd call the baby Charles, of course,'

said he.'

'I have a hunch it will be a boy,' Julia told him. 'I expect Daniel would prefer that, most men do, but it doesn't matter very much whichever it is.'

Charles was now contemplating painting the portrait of his career, Julia with the baby in her arms. He would get it past that damned silly selection committee into Burlington House, where most certainly he would never get Mrs. Tanner, and what was more he had no wish to get Mrs. Tanner. She had been on the telephone this morning because she didn't like her nose in the picture—would you believe it? Born with a nose like a clothes-peg and now when at last it dawned on her that she should have used it for pegging out the clothes, she had the effrontery to blame Charles for it.

They lunched gaily on cold chicken.

There had been an excited letter from the Baroness who was in fine fettle. She had had a miraculous invitation to join the most thrilling shooting party at the shooting box of an Ethiopian Prince. She had written that he was deeply attracted to her ('The silly old fool!' said Charles), and they would be hunting together in the mountains. Although there were fourteen others going to the party, she confided in Griselda that the Prince was giving it entirely for her benefit and was madly in love with her.

'Damned old fool, he's welcome to that one!'

248

said Charles, helping himself to more chicken and ham.

'*Müttchen* has always had romances, and I don't think he is so old really; younger than she is if I remember rightly. It never comes to anything of course, for the men are too clever.'

'If I'd known that one before, it would have saved me many a heartbeat,' Charles commented.

They lingered happily over lunch. Afterwards when they had done with the coffee, they went into the garden pleasant with the mature warmth of September. Charles picked an apple from the tree. Ridiculous as it might seem, although he lived in Kent he had no apple trees in the garden. 'One fruitless old cherry, a gentleman, I think,' he said, 'and a couple of Kentish cobs which do us fine, but a chap can't live on Kentish cobs, can he?' then as they came within sight of the Dower House 'What's happened to Clare?'

'She's gone off on another of her unending visits. She really is odd in that way, you would be surprised the friends she has all over the country.'

'She doesn't strike me as a thrill,' said Charles. 'She is just the sort of woman I get commissioned to paint and not a thing in her. She would be the fit partner for that bank manager of mine, damn the man, he's been going off the deep end again, cold toast is the

249

password.'

'She sent me the most peculiar letter, then disappeared after being back for just one night. I thought she had returned for the winter.'

'She's better away than here. It's nicer without her,' said Charles setting his teeth into a hard apple.

Julia had the feeling of being in an oasis. Of a desert round her being hot, suffocating and surrounding, but here with her father and Griselda she had the sense of happiness. Danger retreated. Fear went away.

'I wish you didn't have to go home tonight,' she said when they returned to tea on the terrace.

'But Daniel will be back so soon. It may even be earlier than you think.'

'He said in his letter two or three days would be the soonest, could be almost this week.'

'When he comes home everything in the garden will be lovely!' Charles was in his most cheerful mood. 'Think what he will say about the baby! I'd ask for a diamond bracelet for that one.'

'Whatever would I do with a diamond bracelet?'

'Pop it when hard times come. They always come back to me some time or other, and then a diamond bracelet would be a lot of help.' He laughed with her.

She waved them from the front door, because

they had to get home early lest Hoggie kicked up a dust. 'Him' had been 'poorly' the last few days. 'Him' liked her to get back early and she had promised she would. They drove away in the creaky old car, and down the drive, letting go with a final toot at the gate. Julia went back to the library, and she had the feeling that the sun was shining less vividly now. The oasis which had been so secure and happy with her own people had dispersed and she was back in the desert again. Afraid.

On the sofa lay the tissue paper and the little white teddy bear; looking at it she knew she should be the happiest person in all the world. Daniel would be home so soon, there would be a baby in April. She went to the mirror over the escritoire and looked at her reflection; she was remembering what Daniel had once said, something she applied to the tired look in her eyes.

> *But one man loved the pilgrim soul in you*
> *And all the sorrows of your changing face.*

★   ★   ★

Daniel will be back soon, she kept telling herself. Nothing matters once he is here.

Two mornings later she woke at seven with a most violent attack of sickness, the worst she had had so far. Last night she had been depressed as she sat over the library fire. The new books had come down from Harrods but had not arrested her interest. Restlessness had made her fidgety and with it there was the sense of catastrophe, something arising from no cause but striking her hard.

She had gone up to bed without drinking the Ovaltine that Mrs. Dawes had brought her last thing; somehow when she got it she could not swallow it. In her room she had felt so bewilderingly ill that she forgot to lock the door behind her. It was strange that ever since Mrs. Dawes had come to her she had locked the door every night, simply because she was afraid to leave it open. She had the idea (she knew it was crazy) that Mrs. Dawes would come in to her, without her glasses, and with those awful eyes watching her. But last night she had not even noticed that she had left it unlocked.

She had crawled into bed falling into an uneasy sleep, which was not a real sleep but like some sort of coma. She woke at seven with the sharp sunlight falling between the curtains, and the sickness with her. She did not believe she had ever felt so bad before. The room spun. Was it for hours or minutes? Was she dozing or awake, or just suffering? She was not conscious of the actual moment when she saw that Mrs. Dawes was standing beside the bed with the morning tea-tray in her hand. Julia heard her speak.

'You are not well, madam?'

'I'm sorry. I—I'm ill. It—it happens most mornings just now, I'm afraid.'

'You should see a doctor, madam.'

When the besetting wave of nausea had passed, Julia spoke again in a pained voice. 'I have seen the doctor. You see, I'm going to have a baby.'

Mrs. Dawes stood there very still.

In that moment it seemed that an almost unbelievable quiet had come into the room, a quiet which accepted both of them into its complete silence. Julia feeling it knew that the sickness was passing; she could see more clearly for the grey haze was leaving her, and the dizziness had gone with it. Mrs. Dawes was very white, it seemed that her face was twitching.

'Is—is something the matter?' Julia asked.

The woman tried to speak, failed, gulped hard and then began again. 'I never had a child,' she said, and her voice was almost a whisper.

She lifted her hand and slowly removed the smoked glasses, holding them between her scrawny fingers. She was staring straight at Julia as she lay there on the frilled white pillow slip, and about those eyes there was something that was tragic. It could be the dead white scar which cut across her face, or the depraved wretchedness of those sunken eyes, which looked as if they had never known youth, yet,

253

for some reason which Julia at the moment could not place, were familiar. Then she heard herself speaking in a voice which she did not recognize as being her own. She was asking the question which had been on her lips several times in the last few hours, and which she had so far dismissed as being absurd. It was no longer absurd.

'Who are you?' she asked.

Yet when the woman spoke, Julia knew she had known the answer deep down within herself for quite a time now. 'I am Theresa.'

'But you are dead? I thought you were dead!'

'That wasn't true. In the accident so many were killed, many hopelessly mutilated, and my bag was lost. I think some other woman died for me and I got away—like this.' Her hand went up to the face where all that beauty had been shattered. 'Please don't be afraid of me any more for I shall never hurt you or Dan. If I had had a child everything could have been so different. If . . .'

She was speaking of the child in the way religious men speak of temples and the good of their cathedrals.

'Why did you come here?' Julia asked. Her heart was making a peculiar noise and the curious thing was that she was not so amazingly surprised as she should have been. 'Daniel believed you were dead.'

'Everyone did. I saw my own name in the

254

paper. To get this job I invented a car accident, for I had to explain my face. I was thrown clear of the train, one of the lucky ones, or was I? For a time I had amnesia and could not tell them who I was; when I had recovered from that I did not want to tell them. I think when I first saw my face I could have died of shame, after being—after being pretty—to be this! It was quite dreadful.'

'You were more than pretty,' said Julia gently. 'I have looked at your portrait so often, and you were very beautiful.'

As if she had not heard what was said, Theresa went on. 'I loved this house. Wetherley is a person, not bricks and mortar, and it can possess one. Lying in that hospital I dreamt of it. I remembered the view across to the Hog's Back and the big dining-room where once Dan and I were so happy. I—tried to forget. It is terrible when you can no longer forget.'

'Why did you not get in touch with him?'

'I could not remember his name then, later when I realized how terribly I had changed, I could not have let him see me. My marriage had broken, and that was my fault, all my own fault. There were things . . .' She turned away with a sudden bitterness, choking down the words. 'Would YOU have got in touch if suddenly you had found yourself to be so hideous?'

Julia thought of the radiant girl in the portrait below and she felt passionately sorry for this

255

poor creature who clasped the scarred face in her two hands. Surely that had had some psychological effect upon her, and had changed her? Yet somewhere in that face there was the faint trace of the other girl, a travesty of what once had been.

She said, 'Theresa, what are you going to do? Daniel may be back any time now, and he has no idea that you are here. We have got to help him, haven't we?'

'I am going away.'

'But you meant to meet him, surely?'

'Yes.' She wiped her eyes and replaced the dark glasses. 'I meant to reproach him. The bitterness became too big for me but today somehow everything is different. I get these moods; they come, but they go again. Perhaps I'm mad. Perhaps I'm demented. I don't know. But this time I am going away and I shall never come back. I promise you that.'

'But why did you come back?'

Theresa spoke slowly and her voice had lost its timbre. 'I wanted money. It is a hard life when you have to earn for yourself and I've never been very strong. I came back to this part of the world because Wetherley has always been a magnet to me. I love it, you see, and one day you will love it the way I do, and be drawn to it and long for it. I wanted to see it again. When that stupid little parson brought the message, I thought fate was on my side and I'd take the job.

It amused me thinking that when Daniel returned he'd find me here and have to pay me an awful lot of money to go away. It just amused me.'

'Oh, Theresa!'

'I don't suppose he has ever told you much about me. Perhaps I hurt him too much. I just don't know. He is the sort of man who can be like a clam.'

'He has never said a thing against you.'

She sank down on to the low chair at the bed-end and rested tiredly against it. 'You ought to know. I drank. All my people drank, it runs in the family. Not just a noggin here and there, because I can't face the world till I AM drunk. I started getting it badly soon after our marriage when I had pneumonia. Then I couldn't give it up. Tried, but couldn't. He should have told you.'

'Daniel is very loyal.'

'I know. When I knew he had married again and I was so hard-up I recognized it as being bigamy. I came back to my house, my own loved house which was not a place to me but a person. I thought it would make me happy but somehow the house has turned against me. I have felt it all the time. I thought the irony of the situation would amuse me, but it made me want to cry. It was no longer a thrill that Daniel would pay anything to be rid of me.' She paused, then she said, 'But I don't care,' and she began to laugh.

The sound of that laughter was discordant; it showed on what a thin thread was suspended that strange mind of hers. It was the screeching of a jay, the rasping of the jackdaw too, and the sound of it actually hurt Julia.

'Don't do that!' she said sharply.

The laughter stopped. There came silence, and now about that twisted face with the flesh looping in faded curves, and grown coarsened from drink, there was something almost pitiful. 'I am going away. I promise you that. If we had had a child everything could have been so different, but we never had one.'

She moved stiffly to the door as though in this short while she had aged considerably.

Julia said, 'My handbag is on the dressing stool where I left it last night. Please open it, Theresa, and take out the notecase. There is about ten pounds in it, all I have, but you cannot go away with nothing and I don't want you to do that. Take the money and write to me from your new address so that I can send you more.'

Theresa had gone to the door and from it she turned, her head flung back just as it was in the portrait downstairs. She was defiant. 'I don't want your damned money,' she said.

Then she had gone.

★   ★   ★

Julia lay still, she dozed for a while and woke feeling better, for it was odd how this malady cleared itself. She remembered Theresa being in this room, or had she dreamt it? It MUST have been a dream! When she went downstairs she would find Mrs. Dawes (not Theresa) getting on with the housework and she would then know that it was an illusion, all part of being sick.

Yet when she dressed and went downstairs, Wetherley was very still. Its silence was ominous, something that told her before she actually knew the truth that she was again alone in the house.

The kitchen was empty, silent and very clean. She called 'Theresa?' knowing for certain now that this had been her name, but there was no reply. She went upstairs to the room that had been Mrs. Marriner's, then had been allotted to the woman who once had herself been mistress of this house. It was a fantastic situation.

There was no reply to Julia's knock and when she tried the handle the door opened. A packed trunk stood on one side, there was an empty whisky bottle on the washstand, and the room reeked with the acrid smell of spirits. The stench made the girl cough. This was the secret that Daniel had kept, and the truth which Mrs. Marriner had tried to swerve from Theresa to Daniel, to deceive Julia. 'Perhaps that would split them,' must have been what Mrs. Marriner had thought, but it hadn't split them.

Clare must have realized who Theresa was; they had talked that night when they went back to the Dower House across the park, and that was why her sister-in-law had written that queer note to Julia. She had not dared ring her up. The allowance which Daniel gave his sister influenced her all the time, and she was naturally careful. 'She should have told me,' Julia thought, 'for this was something I ought to have known.' Today part of her had grown up considerably. She felt a changed person. Older. More sure of herself, for she had matured in the knowledge of Theresa.

The ghost no longer terrified her. She had been right when she had told herself that Wetherley was warm and friendly, a loved house which loved people. Wetherley had never held ghosts, and it had loathed the ghost which came to it. Yet Julia was sorry for Theresa. *I never had a child*, was what she had said, and the tragedy of those words kept on echoing in Julia's own heart.

When she came downstairs she saw that Cathie had come in from hanging tea towels in the garden.

'Wh'r's Mrs. Dawes?' she asked.

'I think she's gone out.'

Cathie nodded as though this was a secret she understood; her eyes were roguish, and she laughed. 'You sm'll it too?' she asked.

Gallantly Julia defended Theresa. Once she had reigned here and Daniel had loved her, now Julia was no longer jealous, nor suspicious, nor anxious. She said, 'I won't have you talking like that, Cathie. You are not to say these things. Mrs. Dawes is out.'

'I'm s'ry, ma'm.' Tears welled into her eyes.

'It's all right, Cathie, don't cry. Only I just can't let you talk this way about the people who are over you.' As she returned into the hall Julia could hear Cathie's raucous sobs (she always made something of a good cry and liked the whole world to know she was having it). Julia went to the library.

For a moment she had thought of telephoning Charles and telling him what had happened; then the new Julia, the girl who had grown up, stopped her. Loyalty to her husband came first. Nobody must know of this save their two selves. Charles would possibly think it rather funny, and although she liked his laughter, now she could not have borne it. Perhaps this was going to be the corner-stone on which fuller marriage to Daniel would be built up. Doubt had gone. She felt secure. Part of her had always known that something dreadful could happen, and she had nursed that absurd premonition; now it had come true. It had ceased in its truth.

She went into the big dining-room with the morning sun falling into it in ripples of mature gold. From over the mantelpiece she saw violet-blue eyes watching her. It was the lovely face of this girl before drink had obsessed her, a legacy handed on by an illness, something too great for her. A beauty which had been hers before she was shocked and deprived and so deeply unhappy. 'She will never return,' Julia thought, 'I know she will never return,' but the girl in the picture had that little amused smile as though there was still much in life that was entertaining. Youth's smile, something Julia had had yesterday, but now she also had grown up.

Cathie was limping into the room with a telegram on the salver, and she was still snivelling. The telegram was from London airport and it came from Daniel. He had caught the first plane this morning and would be with her for lunch.

★   ★   ★

In that moment all that Julia thought about was the food. What was there in the house that Cathie could cook for them? Cathie stopped snivelling. She was wanted again; maybe she would get back to Wetherley to live there for ever. She'd cook a lovely lunch, she said, what about eggs?

It would have to be a meal out of a tin today, after all there should be greater problems than lunch at the moment. There would be so much to talk about, not only the baby which until now

Julia had thought to be the most urgent topic of all, but about Theresa. As she made plans she heard the library telephone ringing. Mrs. Bentley went to it for her and came back alarmed. It was not Daniel as Julia had half expected, it was the police.

'The police?' she asked, and instantly she was on edge again, her hands trembling. 'I'll come.' She went into the library shutting the door behind her and she took up the receiver. 'Yes?' she said, 'it's Mrs. Strong speaking.'

'Surrey police, madam. We understand that until this morning you had a woman in your employ called Mrs. Gertrude Dawes.'

'Yes. She left this morning.'

'Did she leave on foot, madam?'

Amazed, Julia said, 'Yes, of course she did.'

'Has she left her luggage behind her?'

'She has. She will send for it, I am sure,' and then growing more nervous, 'What has happened?'

'A car was taken from the village this morning, a Wolseley, HGI 728. This car has been involved in an accident on the Guildford road.'

'You mean she stole the car?'

'We believe that, madam.'

'Is she badly hurt?'

'She is dead, madam. She came out of the side road with no warning and increased speed. A woman with a brown loose coat; an envelope addressed to Wetherley was in her handbag; her face was scarred, she had iron-grey hair. We understand this woman was a caretaker at Mr. Solomon's at Penshurst, and only last week came into your employ under the name of Gertrude Dawes.'

Cold horror crept up Julia's spine. 'Yes, yes, she did.'

'You know nothing about her, madam? Who she really was? What references did you have?'

'She had some in her bag, I saw no more.' She had not wanted Theresa to die, she could not believe that this had happened, and felt herself going icy cold.

'One of our men will be coming to make inquiries, madam. Mr. Strong is away, we understand. There will also be the question of identification of the body.'

'Identification?' Julia gasped.

The voice was like a machine. 'The body is in the hospital mortuary, madam, the ambulance took her there.'

Julia knew that she was going to faint and gripped the table closer. In a plaintive, childish little voice she said, 'I—I am alone here and not well, because there have been so many upsets this morning. But my husband will be back for lunch. I—I'd rather you saw him,' she whispered into the phone.

'Very good, madam, we'll send a man round.'

He rang off.

Julia pushed back her thick clinging hair from a brow gone damp. She could not identify the body, the horror of the thought made her retch. Daniel would save her from this, surely? But what if he could not save her? What if she *had* to go? The room blurred. When she came round again Cathie and Mrs. Bentley were both with her. Mrs. Bentley was holding a glass of water to her lips.

'Please drink this, madam,' she said humbly.

'I'm all right.' Then as she lay there gradually returning to reality, Julia heard Cathie babbling.

'Them p'lice. The're all m'drers. All m'drers. Me Dad said so. Me Dad knows...'

★   ★   ★

Julia heard the sound of Daniel's car coming up to the front door of Wetherley with the fanlight above it. In a single instant Daniel himself was in the hall and she rushed to him. There was the emotional floodgate opening on security; she need not be afraid any more; she was no longer alone.

'Julia, my darling! My own! God, how ill you look!'

'I'm not ill, Daniel, not really ill.'

She clung to him as they walked across the hall into the library together; there was the familiar scent of his tweed coat, and the

265

exquisite realization of proximity to him; perhaps only now did she realize how tremendously she had wanted him.

They went to the fire, for although the sun was shining brightly there was a sharp wind blowing across the valley and the sky was speckled with storm clouds. The Hog's Back looked close, always a bad sign, but now it did not matter if it poured, for they were together. They sat down, arms about each other.

'Darling, you look so shockingly ill. Whatever has been happening?

She told him first about herself. She brought him a drink and told Cathie to cut sandwiches, for she had already gathered that he had left Sweden very early this morning; there had been a mix-up in his plans, it was that or waiting till tomorrow, and tomorrow seemed to be too far away.

'Let's fly to the south of France, and get the last of the summer there?' he suggested.

Julia shook her head. Everything she had planned to say slipped from her, and out came the secret she could no longer keep. 'I couldn't, Daniel. Not now. I—I'm going to have a baby in April.'

'You never told me!'

'Because I wanted to tell you yourself just now. That's all.'

'But it's wonderful. I hadn't dared to hope. Theresa having no children . . .'

'I know Theresa had no children.'

He didn't listen. 'I'll be sick with fear for you.'

'There's nothing in having a baby, almost everybody does it at some time or another.' She felt superior and surprisingly brave for now she was unafraid. 'Griselda thought she was going to have one, but she isn't. Charles is sick as mud about being a grandfather, but that can't be helped.'

'So this is the great news?'

'It isn't *all* the news.'

Cathie came in with the sandwiches; she brought them to the table beside them and set them down, grinning and murmuring something inarticulate, then she hobbled off again.

'She's crackers,' said Daniel.

'Mrs. Marriner has left.'

'Oh no? Surely not? I'm sorry about that.'

'She's gone. I've got to tell you things, Daniel. I did once mention an anonymous letter to me, something I found at midnight when I went home on the day before our wedding. It was lying on the mat of the cottage. Then one night there was an envelope she had slipped into the books and it was the same writing. Mrs. Marriner sent me that anonymous letter, warning me not to marry you and saying that I would live to regret it.'

'It said that, Julia? But why on earth didn't

you tell me about it?'

'I tried, and I couldn't. I destroyed the letter, but I couldn't help thinking about it. Then when I found the envelope that had been slipped in with directions to Mr. Bass on it, I challenged her. She went at once. She was in love with you.'

Daniel did not deny it. He said, 'I thought she had got over all that nonsense, made sure, and she said she had. It's my fault. I should never have tried to keep her on, but she was so good...' He paused. 'Puck once said, "Lord, what fools these mortals be!" How right he was!'

'You see, Daniel, actually on our wedding day I found out that you had been married before as you know, and that—well, it worried me.'

'But it was all over and done with. There were reasons why I could never feel about Theresa as I did about you.'

'I know. I *do* know. Wetherley betrays its secrets. You and I never got really close because of that secret. You were remote, so was Clare. Don't interrupt me, because this is something I have got to tell you now. One day when I was digging in the new rock garden, I dug up whole lots of empty bottles.'

He made a choking sound, then when he could speak, he said, 'Go on.'

'You'll hate the truth, but I have to tell you. Mrs. Marriner came along and saw the bottles;

she gave me to understand, quite vaguely of course, that you had had them.'

'I?'

'I tell you, Daniel, I know the truth now, but then I didn't. I've got to tell you everything. When Mrs. Marriner went, I slept alone here and it frightened me. I got Cathie in to sleep only because there was no one else, and I simply could not get a new resident, and Cathie, poor lamb, in her own way is a wee bit frightening.'

'I'll say she is!'

'Hoggie happened to hear of somebody in a caretaking job at Penshurst. The woman was a stranger, but Mr. Lucas saw her, and she came here for an interview. Her name was Gertie Dawes, she was middle-aged, looked rather odd and wore dark glasses all the time. She said she had been in a car accident and her face was half-twisted. I didn't like her awfully, and I felt she didn't like me, but she was the only person I could get, so what could I do?'

'You had references, of course?'

'Oh yes, Daniel, and she came here. I thought that somebody was taking the whisky. Then Cathie began to think so, too, and being Cathie, had to tell me. I wanted Mrs. Dawes to stay till you got back, because she was better than nobody. The doctor told me about the baby, and I have been feeling utterly rotten with it, sick in the morning and tired out all day, so that probably that got me down. Clare came back

269

and dined here one night. She left early and Mrs. Dawes took her across the park, you know the deer scare her. Next day she sent me a peculiar letter telling me that I ought to get rid of Mrs. Dawes, and she herself was going away again quite unexpectedly. When she had dined here there had been no mention of anything like that.'

'But why did she go?' There was suspicion in those dark eyes of his, Julia could see it.

'This morning I was very sick, and last night I had forgotten to lock the door. Mrs. Dawes came in and saw me, and when I told her what was the matter, she said rather slowly, *I never had a child!*'

Daniel said not a word, his face was a mask and it had gone ashen.

'I suppose I knew then, and it is difficult to tell you, for all this is something so apart from us, yet we are in it together. She took off her smoked glasses and looked at me; there was something oddly familiar about her, but so different that I had not known before. She was Theresa.'

He was silent a moment, then he said, 'It isn't true. I don't believe a word of it. She died in the train accident. I had her bag and it couldn't have been anybody else.'

'Her bag got mixed up with another woman who was killed, but Theresa was flung clear. She had amnesia, was in hospital for months, and when she remembered it was too late.'

'I can't believe it.'

'Daniel, they were the same eyes. She told me about her drinking. She knew where the key to the cupboard was, your key, I mean. That was how she got at it.'

'She told you about it?'

'Yes, and that you had promised never to give her away.'

He hid his face in his hands and then shuddered as though he would shake off a memory that still had the power to hurt him. 'Go on,' he said.

'Theresa wanted money. She adored this house, I think the house brought her back, the thought of blackmail as well, but when she knew about the baby she went of her own free will. She would not take the money that I offered her, she had gone before I could get up.'

Slowly he said, 'We have got to find where she is, Julia. She does such crazy things, especially when she has been drinking, and she always took a lot in the night so that she would be cocky and brave enough to face the new day. She'd do anything.'

Julia nodded. 'Half an hour ago the Surrey police rang through. She went into the village and stole a car to get away in. I suppose she just wanted to get away, poor thing! She drove badly.'

'She always did. You mean there was an

271

accident?'

'She's dead, Daniel.'

He hid his face again for a moment, and when he took his hands away and put his arms about her, his eyes were clearer. 'I suppose that had to be.'

'They want me to go to the mortuary to identify her, but I couldn't do it, Daniel, I just couldn't do it.'

'It looks as if it was a good thing I came home. Of course you won't do it.'

She began to cry and he took her into his arms like a baby. Now she could collapse and there was something very satisfying in the thought. He kissed her again and again, and when she was quieter he telephoned the police and his solicitor.

They ate a casual lunch of tinned tongue, no longer at opposite ends of the table but sitting side by side because every little while she wanted to touch him and be sure he was there. Charles rang up as they were finishing.

'Daniel's back,' Julia cried excitedly.

He said, 'Then everything in the garden's lovely. There's nothing more to worry about.'

'Nothing,' she agreed, and there was a little catch in her voice.

'What does he think of Gertie Dawes?'

It seemed funny that he should ask that. It was even funnier that acting on the spur of the moment she should gloss over the whole thing.

'Oh, she's left us. We'll have to get somebody else.'

She couldn't explain more now. She doubted if she ever would explain everything, and she only hoped that the inquest would cover it. She laid down the receiver and turned back to Daniel. 'Darling,' she said, 'so much has happened. I feel quite different. Awfully different. I believe I've grown up at last.'